SWEET BRUTALITY

A DARK MAFIA ROMANCE

ZOE BLAKE

SWEET BRUTALITY

A DARK MAFIA ROMANCE

By Zoe Blake

* * *

Published by Stormy Night Publications and Design, LLC.
www.StormyNightPublications.com
Blake, Zoe
Sweet Brutality
Cover Design by Dark City Designs
Photographer: Wander Aquilar

CONTENTS

CHAPTER 1

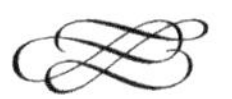

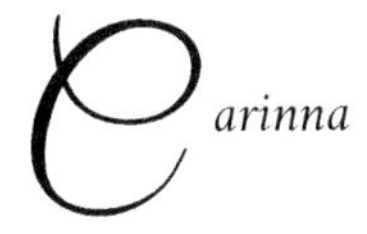

arinna

It was the never-ending shift from hell.

Usually I didn't mind bartending for my rent money. It was a decent job with great tips and had a super flexible schedule that fit around my pastry classes.

But not tonight… tonight it was a nightmare.

I was only an hour into my shift, and I'd already cut my finger slicing lemons, and some asshole had tipped his beer over on the bar and ruined my favorite pair of black leather leggings. It certainly didn't help that I was wearing the most uncomfortable and revealing leather corset top ever made. I placed my hands on either side of my boobs and yanked it up. What had I been thinking? I needed tips, but not bad enough to display the girls on a silver platter for the idiots who came to this bar.

I glanced at the cash register clock.

Just six more hours to go.

Thankfully, I wasn't closing tonight, so I could clock out at midnight.

The moment I got home, I was taking this torture trap of a top off and getting a nice, long, hot shower. The thought of my favorite author's latest fabulously smutty book uploaded on my Kindle waiting for me made me smile. Yep, a dark and kinky read was the closest I'd been to having a boyfriend over the last four hundred and thirty-two days, but who was counting? Besides, boyfriends were a nuisance. I was already in my mid-twenties and I'd yet to meet a guy who wasn't just a glorified man-baby. They usually needed constant attention, not to mention teaching them how to dress and act properly so they didn't embarrass you in front of your friends. The worst ones barely knew how to feed themselves, let alone enough to appreciate dining in a fine restaurant. Nope, I was better off staying in a committed relationship with my Kindle bad boy toys.

Thinking of bad boys brought to mind Maxim, the man who'd confronted me and my best friend Dylan outside my apartment earlier today.

The man had practically screamed dirty, sexy, hot.

I had opened my apartment door to find a wall of muscle in an Armani suit blocking the way. He'd had the audacity to inform Dylan he had changed the locks without her permission. He'd then had the arrogance to chastise us both for our attire—Dylan for being wrapped in a towel and me for wearing a T-shirt and silk sleep shorts. I could almost still hear his rumbly, rough voice as he glared at me, scolding me like I was a rebellious teenager.

He turned to me. "You as well. You should know better than to walk around naked." He motioned toward my apartment door with his head. "Get back inside and cover yourself."

Placing my fists on my hips, I fired back, "Who the hell do you think you are? And I am not naked!"

Maxim placed a hand high on the wall and leaned over me. "I'm the man who is going to strip that skimpy piece of fabric you call an outfit off your body and spank your ass red if you don't obey me this instant."

EVERY INCH of my skin prickled with awareness. It was as if he were standing behind me, instead of just being a heated memory. His breath on my neck. His fingertips running up and down my exposed arms. His mouth on my—holy hell, I needed to stop thinking about him!

It didn't take a genius to tell he was the type of man who would bend a girl over a table, flip her skirt up, and pound into her till she screamed in ecstasy, giving her the best sex of her life. But fortunately, I could also tell he was the kind of man who would give a girl a quick caress on the cheek and a seductive wink afterward before he casually walked away, forgetting her name. If he had bothered to remember it in the first place.

Yep, there was practically a halo of red flags flapping all around him and I was going to stay far, far away. Not that there was ever a chance in hell I'd see him again.

"Hey! You! Gimme a beer!"

I glanced at the customer who'd just shouted at me. He was poorly dressed in a stained T-shirt and an incorrectly buttoned flannel. I could practically smell the stale beer on his breath. Usually he wouldn't have gotten past the front door, but our bouncer was out sick tonight. The assistant manager was paying more attention to a blonde with a big rack than he was to who was strolling into the bar. He was useless.

I nodded in Flannel Guy's direction. "One sec." Then I

motioned with my head for my bar back, Timmy, to come over.

He approached, carrying a trash can full of empty beer bottles and discarded cocktail napkins. "What's up, Carinna?"

Reaching for a cocktail shaker, I filled it with ice while I kept my gaze straight ahead. "Grab the GM. I think that guy who just arrived has been overserved. There's no way I'm giving him a beer."

Timmy handed me a bottle of Belvedere Vodka for the martini I was making as he also kept his gaze averted. We knew better than to alert a customer we were discussing them. "The guy in the flannel?"

I capped the cocktail shaker and held it aloft over my right shoulder as I shook it vigorously while reaching for a martini glass with my left hand. "Yup. That's the one."

"On it." He held the trash can high as he exited the bar area and made his way to the back of the house to find the general manager.

It would be my job to keep Flannel Guy calm and occupied until help arrived.

I placed the martini in front of the woman I was serving and took her credit card to start a tab.

Flannel Guy slammed his flat palm on the bar. "Hey, bitch! I said I want a beer."

I printed out the receipt for the martini and placed it in a pint glass with the credit card and put it on a shelf over the cash register. Ignoring his slur, I kept my voice calm and upbeat. "Sorry for the wait. I have a few customers ahead of you, sir. It will be just a moment."

Where the hell was the manager?

I filled a rocks glass with ice and snatched the Tanqueray Gin from the back bar. Picking up the soda gun, I hit the tonic button as I counted out an ounce and a half of gin as I poured. After a quick scan of the bar, I realized my cut limes were in a container by Flannel Guy. Damn.

Dealing with unruly customers was part of the job, but it always made me nervous. Especially when I was dressed like I should be holding a whip and a bottle of lube. Again, I yanked on my leather corset top, pulling it as high over my boobs as I could before I approached that end of the bar. Flannel Guy's head was turned in the other direction, so the timing was perfect.

I extended my arm and grabbed the small plastic container of limes. Just as I was making a clean getaway, a steely grip wrapped around my wrist. Before I could react, Flannel Guy jerked hard on my arm. My upper body slammed forward as my stomach crashed into the sharp edge of the bar, knocking the breath out of my lungs. I opened my mouth to scream for help, but nothing came out.

Terrified, I looked up to see Flannel Guy raise his arm into the air, fist closed. "Bitch, I'm gonna—"

I squeezed my eyes shut and braced for the punch I knew was coming.

But no punch came.

I opened my eyes in time to see Flannel Guy's head get slammed down onto the bar by a large hand covered in tattoos. Blood gushed from the guy's now-broken nose. He cried out in pain as he released my wrist.

I staggered backward to safety. Lifting my head, I opened my mouth to thank my rescuer and froze. For the second time that day, all the breath left my body.

My gaze clashed with a pair of furious emerald eyes.

Maxim had found me.

CHAPTER 2

arinna

The shouts and cries of all the bar patrons receded to nothing more than a dull drumming in the back of my mind as I stared at Maxim.

He had changed out of his dark Armani suit but still looked intimidating as fuck, dressed in a black cashmere sweater and jeans. His sleeves were rolled up, exposing muscular forearms covered in bright tattoos. They were a macabre collection of skulls, daggers, drops of blood, and religious themes. My gaze then traveled down to his hands, which were also covered in evil-looking ink, as they still pinned drunk Flannel Guy's face to the bar.

Seeing the manager approach from over Maxim's shoulder with a furious scowl on his face, I raised a placating hand. "Stop. You can't do that!"

Maxim's eyes narrowed as his upper lip lifted in a snarl. Ignoring my plea, he twisted his hand in Flannel Guy's hair and wrenched him upward. Blood flowed from the man's broken nose down the front of his dirty T-shirt. Maxim then gave the man a ruthless shake. "Apologize to the lady."

The man ran his shirtsleeve under his nose, smearing blood across his unshaven cheek. He muttered something unintelligible.

Choosing to assume the man apologized, I nodded my head vigorously as I waved both hands in front of me. "Fine. It's fine. I accept your apology."

My general manager was now standing behind Maxim. His neck stretched all the way back as he tried to reconcile his small five foot four, slightly pudgy frame to Maxim's clearly well over six foot frame of hard muscle. Choosing an easier target, his beady eyes swung my way. "Carinna! If you don't get control of your friend now, you're fired."

Control him?

The man is like a junkyard dog off his leash.

How the hell am I supposed to control him?

Before I could respond to the GM's threat, Maxim pivoted. Still holding Flannel Guy by the hair like some soiled rag doll, Maxim's head tilted to the right as he surveyed my GM. One eyebrow lifted. His voice was dark honey as he asked, "Do you want to be next?"

Despite Maxim's heavy Russian accent, there was no doubt my manager understood the threat. His mouth opened and closed several times without making a sound. Finally he shook his head, his double chin wobbling with the effort. "No… no."

Maxim tightened his grip on Flannel Guy. "If I ever lay eyes on you again, I'll rip your heart out through your mouth. Do you understand me?"

The man's sputtered reply sent droplets of blood flying over the GM's suit. "Yes! I'm sorry. I'll leave. You'll never see me again."

Maxim nodded before releasing his grip and allowing the man to stumble over toward the GM. Both men weaved and swayed before being helped by Timmy.

"You should not have let this garbage into your bar. Take care of it."

Both Timmy and my GM struggled to lead Flannel Guy away.

My relief at the situation being defused was short-lived.

Maxim turned to face me.

I took a step back, then another, retreating to the far end of the bar.

He raised his arm and pointed to the spot in front of him. "Carinna, get over here."

With his accent, he rolled the harsh C in my name till it sounded like the purr of a lion. A very dangerous lion who looked like he could swallow me in one bite and not even choke on my bones.

I snatched up a bar towel and wiped the already clean bar surface near me. "Sorry, I can't. I have customers," I called over my shoulder, refusing to make eye contact with him. I raised my chin in a curt nod to the customer nearest me. "What can I get you?"

The customer looked from me to Maxim and back again. "Nothing. I'm good."

Doing everything in my power to try to ignore the pillar of furious rage standing a few feet away, I tried again. "How about you?" I asked, nodding to another nearby customer.

Out of the corner of my eye, I saw Maxim tilt his head to the right in what I was fast learning was a sign of trouble. "Carinna." His voice held more than a hint of warning.

I tapped a rapid staccato on the bar with the tips of my fingers. "Come on, buddy. I don't have all day. What can I get you? A beer? Whiskey? What?"

Just like the last one, this customer glanced from me to

Maxim, before backing away from the bar. One by one my customers drifted away.

I inhaled deeply through my nose. A vain attempt to gather my courage before turning to face Maxim.

He had crossed his arms over his chest. His brow lowered as his lips tightened in a thin line. "I am out of patience."

Out of patience?

At what part of this had he been showing patience?

I twisted the bar towel between my fists. "Look, thanks for your help, but I have to get back to work."

Maxim stood near the service entrance to the bar. Keeping his hard gaze on me, he reached down and swung the heavy bar top upward. There was a crash, then the tinkle of broken glass as the bar top slammed against the wall, sending several martini glasses on a nearby shelf crashing to the floor.

He stepped forward, allowing the bar top to fall back into place with a deafening clatter, caging us both in behind the bar.

My eyes widened as he approached, knowing there was no escape.

He placed both hands on the bar on either side of me. He leaned down. The stubble on his jaw brushed my cheek as he whispered into my ear. "In the future, if you make me call your name twice, I will take you over my knee. Do you understand me?"

I blinked several times. This was the second time today this man had threatened to spank me. The fact my stomach flipped at the thought each time meant there was something seriously wrong with me. Still, that was a thought for later, when I was safe in my bed under the covers with my Kindle. Not now when I was face-to-face with a tattooed monster of a man who seemed to be following me.

The bar glassware stored just below the bar rattled as I

shifted, trying to put at least a few inches between us. "What are you doing here?" I demanded.

Without answering my question, he motioned with his hand and ordered, "Get your things. We're leaving."

Both my eyebrows rose as I crossed my arms under my chest. "The hell we are. I'm not going anywhere with you."

His eyes sparked viridian fire as they focused on my cleavage.

With a gasp, I realized my crossed arms had pushed my breasts up till my nipples were practically popping out over the top of the corset. I yanked on my top, trying to pull it as high as I could over my boobs. Stupid corset was going straight into the trash when I got home. I lifted the hand holding the bar towel up to my chest for good measure.

Maxim wrapped his fingers around my wrist and jerked me against his chest. He then speared his fingers into my hair and pulled my head back, holding it tight so I couldn't turn away. "You have played the whore long enough tonight. You're leaving with me. Now." The last word was ground out through clenched teeth.

Whore?

Whore!

Did he just freaking call me a whore?

Without a thought for the repercussions, I drew back my free hand and slapped him hard across the cheek.

Maxim's head turned to the side as he absorbed the strike. When he turned back to face me, a ghost of a smile teased his lips.

It was terrifying.

He leaned down and said nothing for what felt like a full minute. His lips skimmed mine, breathing in my air, like a demon stealing the breath from my body. He opened his mouth and pulled my lower lip in, then sank his sharp teeth into the soft flesh. His hard grip on my head prevented me from pulling away. I whimpered as I tasted the coppery tang of blood.

Finally, he released my lip. He licked the wound he had created then rasped against my mouth, "You'll learn what a mistake that was later—when I get you alone."

I couldn't be certain, but I honestly thought I blacked out, just for a second, from pure fear. He sounded like an angry father admonishing a misbehaving child about the punishment they would receive when they got home.

In a last-ditch effort to extricate myself from this mess, I insisted, "You can't just drag me out of here in front of all these people."

"Watch me."

"Someone will stop you."

His lips lifted at the corner. "No—they won't."

"I'll call the police."

His eyebrow rose. "You think I'm afraid of American police?"

This was insane. He couldn't honestly think to get away with just kidnapping me out of a public bar. Then I remembered this was the man who had changed my friend's locks without even asking her permission. Clearly, these Russian men didn't think the rules applied to them.

Feeling lightheaded, I tried to stand my ground. "I'm not going anywhere with you."

He took a step back.

I breathed a sigh of relief.

Then he pulled his sweater over his head.

Jesus, Mary, and Joseph.

The man wasn't just inked over every inch of hard muscle; he was pierced, as in *pierced.* He had a barbell piercing through each nipple and three more barbells going up each pectoral. At the base of his neck, there was a heavy-looking silver captive bead ring. As if it were a hook for a damn leash.

Holy shit!

I opened my mouth to—what? Cry out? Scream? Moan? All I could do was utter a helpless squeak.

Maxim stepped close and pulled the sweater over my head, covering my exposed breasts. I closed my eyes and inhaled the scent of his cologne as the warmth from his body, still trapped within the cashmere, caressed my own.

Before I could object or, at the very least, put my arms through the sleeves, he bent low and tossed me over his shoulder. With my arms trapped, all I could do was cry out in vain. "Put me down!"

Maxim gave my ass a sharp, stinging slap. "No."

I called out to Timmy, who was standing nearby. "Are you just going to let him carry me away?"

Timmy gestured to Maxim. "Do you see the size of him?"

Maxim gestured to the area under the cash register. "Is that her purse?"

Timmy rushed to grab it and handed it to Maxim.

Well, isn't he just the fucking helpful friend?

Maxim carried me with ease through the bar. The patrons actually moved aside to create a pathway for him. No one raised so much as a pinky to help me despite my cries and pleas. So much for chivalry.

There was a rush of cold air as Maxim kicked the exit door open. It slammed shut after us with a startling finality. The dark winter night closed around me.

I was alone with the Russian monster.

CHAPTER 3

axim

I LET OUT A LONG, frosty breath, but the chilled air did nothing to cool my rage.

To see her parading in front of those men with barely anything covering her tits made me want to murder each and every man in that bar. There was no excuse for putting herself on display like that, none at all. Obviously, whatever shit excuse for a man she belonged to wasn't doing his job to keep her in line. I didn't give a fuck if she belonged to someone else. A man who couldn't rein in his woman deserved to lose her. And this woman clearly needed the firm hand of a man's protection. My hand.

I dug into my jeans pocket for the car keys as I marched over to the Mercedes-Benz I had borrowed from Dimitri while I was in town, with Carinna still squirming and protesting on my shoulder. I had deliberately parked on the far side of the lot, in an area partially concealed by trees. An old habit. I didn't want to make it easy for anyone to see my license plate or exact car model.

"Put me down, you bastard degenerate bastard!"

I chuckled. "You called me bastard twice."

"That's because you're twice the bastard!" she fired back without hesitation.

Damn, I loved a woman with a little fire in her belly.

"I'll scream," she warned.

I scanned the dark and desolate parking lot as I walked around my metallic silver car and popped the trunk. "Go ahead."

Carinna shifted. Her chin bumped the side of my head as she maneuvered to see behind her. "Don't you even fucking think about putting me in that trunk!"

If I wanted to put her in the trunk, I would put her curvy ass in the trunk and there was nothing she could do about it. As it so happened, I didn't want to be deprived of her colorful rhetoric. So I had no intention of forcing her to ride in the trunk. I placed her on her feet.

Carinna reached for the hem of my sweater.

My eyes narrowed. "Take it off and see what happens."

She paused before her eyes also narrowed. Tightening her lips into a scowl, she drew the sweater over her head and tossed it onto the muddy parking lot tarmac.

I ran the tip of my tongue over the front of my teeth as I met her defiant stare. "And that's three."

She crossed her arms under her breasts before seeing my sharpened gaze and realizing her error. She placed one arm over her chest and crossed the other to rest her hand on her shoulder. "Three what?"

"Punishments."

Carinna let out a huff of air. It hung heavily before her in a misty cloud, reminding me I needed to get her inside and warm… preferably in a bed. My bed.

Carinna then scowled at me as she hoisted the top by the sides in a fruitless effort to cover her more than ample charms. Staring at the deep V of her cleavage, I wondered if her nipples were pierced. Probably not. That would be something I would need to rectify soon. Pierced nipples were way more sensitive to the touch. Perhaps I would make her get tiny hoops I could attach a small leash to. I shifted as I ran the base of my palm over my growing cock as it strained against the tight denim of my jeans. Later.

"Punishments? You can't be serious. I'm not some child you can take over your knee! I'm a grown-ass woman!"

I grabbed her chin and tilted her head back. It was becoming harder and harder to keep my temper with her. "A *grown-ass woman* would know not to parade around naked in front of a bunch of *grown-ass men*."

She stamped her foot as she tossed her head to the side, breaking my grip. "For the last time, I am not parading around naked! Just because you don't like how I dress doesn't give you the right to—"

"Enough!" I roared as I slammed the trunk lid down.

Her eyes widened. Turning, she tried to bolt.

I snatched at the crimson corset ribbons that trailed down the middle of her back. She jerked to a halt. I dragged her toward me for a few steps before roughly turning her around. Without saying a word, I wrapped my hands around her waist and lifted her onto the top of the trunk.

Placing my palms on the inside of her knees, I forced her legs open and stepped between them. Spearing my fingers into her hair, I pulled her head forward. "You want to dress like a little whore? I'll treat you like one."

I swallowed her outraged protest as my mouth claimed hers. My tongue pushed inside her sweet mouth as I forced my hand down the inside of her corset. I ruthlessly pulled it down, exposing both of her breasts. Breaking free of our kiss, I yanked on her hair. Her head fell back as her chest pushed out. Her dusky pink nipples were pebble hard from the cool night air. I used the top bead of my silver barbell tongue piercing to tease the sensitive flesh.

Her small hands pushed at my shoulders as she pleaded, "Stop! Let me go!"

I licked the inside curve of one heavy breast. "What's the matter? Don't like the consequences of baring your tits to a room full of men?"

"Fuck you!" she fired back as she raised her leg to try to use her heel against my hip to dislodge me.

I grabbed her knee and held it high as I sank my teeth into the soft flesh of the top of her breast. Not enough to break the skin, but just enough to mark her. "Gladly. How much for a quick fuck in the parking lot?"

Carinna screamed in outrage as she struggled to evade my grasp. It was useless. There wasn't a power on this earth that could pry my hands off her.

Using my grip on her hair, I wrenched her off the car and positioned her facedown over the back of the trunk. I caressed my palm over her hip to cup her ass. She rose up on her toes as I gave her right cheek a hard squeeze through the flimsy fabric of her leggings. Placing my fingers into the waistband, I yanked the leggings down, baring her ass.

"Please!" begged Carinna as her arms stretched over the cold metal of the car as if she were trying to claw away from me.

I moved my hand in a circle over her exposed flesh before raising it high to deliver a single stinging slap.

Carinna cried out.

I watched as her chilled, pale skin blossomed into a beautiful shade of dark pink in the shape of my hand. "What's the matter, baby? Don't like being treated like a dirty little whore?"

Her dark brown eyes looked like hard chips of black diamond as she flashed an angry look over her shoulder. "No, damn you!"

Using the side of my boot, I kicked her legs open wider. I ran two fingers along the thin seam of her purple thong panties before tracing the outline of her pussy lips. The stillness of the winter's night allowed me easily to hear Carinna's harsh inhale. I pushed one fingertip inside of her wet warmth.

I ran my lips over the top of her shoulder to flick the tip of my tongue against her earlobe. "I think you're a liar." I thrust my finger in deeper.

Fuck, she was tight, almost virginal tight.

My cock thickened at the thought of sinking deep inside her hot sheath. "Say it," I demanded as I added a second finger inside of her. "Say you're my naughty little whore."

She pounded her fist on the car. "Fuck you."

I reached for my belt buckle, brushing my knuckles against her bare ass. "That can be arranged."

I had no intention of fucking her in a cold parking lot. I would wait till I got her home. Right now, she needed to be taught a lesson.

"Wait!" cried out Carinna.

"No, say it. Say you're my little whore," I demanded as I thrust my fingers in and out of her grasping pussy. A dark and twisted emotion sprang to life inside of me. I'd never been into degradation kink, but there was just something about this woman that made me want to slap her ass and call her my own little whore as I plowed into her. That wasn't nearly as startling as another driving need to cradle her in my arms and call her my sweet babygirl.

In my line of work, you had to be a quick judge of character. It was immediately apparent when I first met her in the hallway of her apartment building that Carinna was an innocent playing at being tough and in control. What else explained her foolish attempt to protect her friend against someone like me?

I still remembered my primal reaction to her standing in that hallway earlier today, daring to defy me. A little mouse challenging a lion. I had wanted to pick her up and put her in my pocket. She was so adorably indignant. While I'd had business to attend to in that moment, it was a foregone conclusion I would track her down later. I had wanted to see those golden sparks fly out of her velvet brown eyes again.

Truth be told, I wanted to provoke her into an argument, just to give myself an excuse to put her over my knee and bare that cute, curvy ass of hers. Never had I imagined she would give me such cause as to be wearing next to nothing as she traipsed from one end of the bar to the other, baring herself for paltry beer tips. And I planned to take *full* advantage of her.

I flicked open the button and lowered the zipper to my jeans. I know she heard the muffled metallic clicks because her breathing stopped. I pushed my fingers in deep as I used the pad of my thumb to tease her tightly puckered asshole. A hint of dark deeds to come. "Admit you like this."

Her head lolled from side to side. "I don't."

"Your body tells me otherwise."

I scissored my fingers deep inside of her. Carinna rose up on her toes and groaned.

"Admit you like it rough and dirty, and I'll let you go." *For now.*

She glared at me through the tangled strands of her honey-brown hair. "I hate you."

"Good. Hold on to that hate. I want you to grasp it tightly till you can feel the heat of your own wrath warming your heart. I want you to seethe with hatred. I want your blood to boil within your veins at the mere thought of me. I want your fingers to curl into claws at the sight of me." I fisted her hair and turned her head to the side so she could feel the full power of my gaze. "You know why, babygirl?"

Her eyes scanned my face. She wet her full lips before choking out a whispered, "No, why?"

"Because I'm going to enjoy throwing you down onto a bed and hate-fucking you till you don't know your own name. I want to feel your heated blood pulse around my cock. I want your claws to tear down my back as I drive into you over and over and over again until you beg me for mercy."

She gasped as her eyes filled with tears. "Oh, my God."

I released her hair and smoothed it back over her skull. "God can't save you now."

Her pussy clenched around my fingers, letting me know she craved the sensual dark side of passion as much as I did. Maybe I had finally met my match. What man didn't want a sweet innocent they could turn into their own personal little whore in the bedroom?

Her bottom lip was still swollen from where I had bitten it. I ran my tongue over it. "Don't make me ask you again. Tell me what I want to hear, or I'll show you just what a heartless bastard I can be."

Carinna whimpered.

I applied more pressure on the pad of my thumb, pushing into her reluctant asshole to the first knuckle as I leaned the weight of my body over hers.

"I'm your dirty little whore," she whispered.

And with those words, she sealed her fate.

CHAPTER 4

arinna

I COULDN'T LET this happen.

Could I?

No! Of course not.

I wasn't the type of girl who would let a tattooed and pierced beast of a man I barely knew fuck me on the trunk of his car in a freaking parking lot.

So why was I finding this all so unbelievably hot? There was no denying it. My pussy was practically dripping down his fingers. There was just something about his gruff, guttural Russian accent. When he called me his dirty little whore, all while his thick fingers thrust inside me, I had to bite my lip to keep from begging him to fuck me.

And Jesus, the feeling of his pierced tongue on my nipple? I practically came the moment I realized what was happening. *If he's pierced on his chest and his tongue, does that mean his...*

oh, God. Don't think about it or I'll beg him to fuck me like the whore he's accusing me of being.

I took a deep breath. *Don't focus on him or his hands or the feel of his heavy muscled weight pressing down on my back.* I needed to focus on my anger, on my hatred of him.

I'm going to enjoy throwing you down onto a bed and hate-fucking you till you don't know your own name.

Dammit, why was that such a turn-on?

I was going to need some serious therapy I couldn't afford, probably for years, to get over this encounter with Maxim.

Before I humiliated myself any further, there was a shriek of drunken laughter and the muffled sound of music as the bar door swung open and a group of patrons stumbled out. We were across the parking lot shielded by his car and a small copse of trees, but that didn't stop me from crying out in alarm.

Maxim cursed low in Russian.

Seizing me by the shoulders, he turned me around and crushed me against his naked chest as I pulled my leggings back up over my waist.

Somehow, despite the evening chill, he radiated heat. It figured. He was obviously half demon, and this was proof. His arm wrapped protectively around my back as he used his hand to press my head into his shoulder. Using his other free hand, he popped the trunk, which shielded us further. Reaching into his duffle bag, he pulled free a dark gray hoodie. It had a large gold and red embroidered emblem on the front with a red star, oak leaves, and a soccer ball with Cyrillic writing across the top. It looked to be some sort of sports team.

"Arms up," he commanded.

I started to obey, then stopped, covering my breasts

instead. My useless corset top was wrapped low around my waist.

He tilted his head to the right. "Carinna." There it was again, that rough warning tone.

With a sigh, I obeyed. He pulled the hoodie down over my head, this time allowing me to place my arms in the sleeves. When he was finished, I hugged the soft, warm, cologne-scented material to my body, hating yet loving the cozy sense of warmth and protection I immediately felt.

Without saying a word, he turned me around and lifted the hem of the hoodie. My body was jerked backward as he yanked on the corset ribbons. "Ow!" I protested.

"No *ow*. I will show you real *ow* later," he darkly threatened as he pulled the offensive corset off me and tossed it into the bushes.

He then reached into the trunk and pulled out a long-sleeved T-shirt from the same bag and threw it over his head. I was almost sorry to see his naked chest covered. In the dim lighting of the parking lot, I hadn't had time really to make out the myriad colorful, yet sinister-looking tattoos that spanned his chest and arms.

I crossed my arms over my chest. There was an awkward heartbeat of silence. It felt like I was back in high school, not knowing what to do after hooking up with a boy at a weekend party and then seeing him again at school the following Monday. "So what happens now? You going to take me out to the desert to kill me and bury my body?"

Maxim frowned and gestured to the twinkling lights of the high-rise building skyline. "We are in Chicago. There are no deserts. Besides, the ground is too hard in winter to bury a body properly."

I blinked several times. That's what I got for asking a snarky question, I guess.

He chucked me under the chin. "Now, we go home and get warm."

I inhaled a sigh of relief. Whatever this was, it was finally over. I would unpack what had happened later over a bottle of wine with Dylan. I reached for my purse, which he had dropped inside his trunk.

He slapped my hand away. "What are you doing?"

"Grabbing my purse, I need my car keys."

"Which car is yours?"

I scanned the parking lot, then pointed. "That one."

Maxim followed my arm, then burst out laughing.

I placed my hands on my hips. "What?"

"What is that, an early '90s Toyota Camry? That is barely over a hundred horsepower. You are joking, no?"

"No, I'm not *joking*. And it's a 1994, thank you very much," I sneered as I mimicked his heavy Russian accent, hurt that he would laugh at my car. I mean, sure, it was a slightly rusted 1994 Toyota Camry in an unfortunate shade of pea green, but it got me where I needed to go and was completely paid off. "Don't make fun of Lucy."

"Lucy?"

I gestured impatiently in the direction of my car. "Yes, Lucy. My car."

He raised one eyebrow. "You named your car Lucy?"

The car was named Lucy because there was a Beatles tape stuck in the cassette player that only played 'Lucy In the Sky with Diamonds' repeatedly, but I wasn't about to tell him that little detail.

I reached into the trunk to try to get my purse again. "Just give me my purse."

He wrapped his fingers around my wrist and pulled my arm back. He then slammed the trunk closed. "No."

"No. No. No. That is all you ever say. Don't you know any other English words?"

He leaned in close. "I know plenty of English words. Lick. Fuck. Wet. Hot. Cock. Cunt."

My cheeks flamed as I took a step back. "That's not what I meant."

Maxim crossed by my side and opened the passenger door of his car. "Get in the car before I fuck you in front of those people over there."

"You wouldn't dare!"

"Try me."

"Why won't you just let me leave in my own car?"

"Because *that* car is a death trap on wheels that is barely better than a broken-down bicycle and you're not allowed to drive it. My car is a Mercedes-Benz S-Class, top of the line with over six hundred horsepower. My car would eat your car as a snack."

Ugh, men and their cars.

"You're a car snob."

"When it comes to comparing what I drive to *that*? Yes, I am. Now get in."

"You're not talking sense. Besides, I'm not leaving my car here. Someone will steal it."

Maxim laughed. "Trust me, babygirl. No one is stealing that piece of crap."

"You're a real bastard, you know that?"

"So you keep telling me. Although the news will come as a shock to my mother and father," he teased.

"I'm not sure you have a mother and father. You were probably just spawned from the depths of hell along with the other demons."

He left his post by the passenger door and stalked toward me. I backed around the car, trying to avoid him. Finally, I had circled the entire car till my ass bumped into the passenger door. Maxim gripped the top of the door and leaned over me. "If I am a demon, are you so sure you should test me this way?"

Ignoring his taunt, I stood my ground. "I'm not leaving my car here."

Grumbling something under his breath about stubborn American women, Maxim reached into his back pocket and pulled out his phone. He dialed quickly and then spoke in rapid Russian. He put the phone back in his pocket. "There. Are you happy now? We can leave."

I threw up my hands. "Um, hello? I don't speak Russian. For all I know, you just sold my car."

His lips twirled up in a smile. "Yes, I sold it. For a gum wrapper and an old sock."

"Not funny."

"One of my men is going to take care of it. Now get in the car."

"Won't he need the keys?"

"No."

"Why not?"

"Because he has a special set of skills that don't require keys to enter cars."

One of his men, more likely a *henchman*!

Maxim sighed. "Carinna, my patience is at an end."

I glanced between him and my car. The thing only started half the time when it was this cold. I desperately wanted to get home and get into a nice hot shower and open a bottle of wine so I could unpack all that had just happened. Besides, he had locked my keys in the trunk. I could try to make a run for it back into the bar, but I already knew no one in there would raise a finger to help me. Resigned to my fate, I still tried to get a little of my own back. "Say please."

"What?" he growled.

"Say please."

"*Please*, get in the car."

"Fine, but only because you asked nicely."

I slid into the passenger seat. Before closing the door, Maxim leaned in. "I'm going to remember your *please* rule."

My cheeks flamed even hotter. Why did everything he said sound like a sexual threat?

He slammed the door shut and walked around the car to the driver's side door.

This is fine.

Everything is going to be fine.

I mean, I was in a car with a big, scary Russian dude who just threatened to fuck me in a public parking lot like a whore, but yuuupp, everything was going to be fine. I would let him give me a ride home, then I would sprint into my apartment and bar the door and wait for Dylan to return from her date with Oliver. The moment she did, I would apologize for trying to convince her to go out with that Russian guy, Ivan, because I thought it would be a romantic adventure. Holy shit, had I been wrong!

There was nothing romantic or adventurous about these Russian men.

They were big and scary as fuck, and I wanted nothing to do with him.

* * *

We rode in silence until his car pulled up out front of my apartment. It irked me a little that he didn't need to even ask where I lived. I still didn't know why he showed up at my bar tonight, but that would have to be a question that went unanswered. There was no way I was prolonging this a minute longer than necessary.

I opened the car door before he had even come to a complete stop. "Thanks! Just pop the trunk and I'll grab my purse."

Maxim parked the car and opened the driver's side door.

I objected. "You don't have to get out. I can just grab my purse."

He used his key fob to pop the trunk. Before I could reach in, he grabbed my purse and his duffle bag. Without saying a word, he closed the trunk and locked the car before wrapping his hand tightly around my upper arm. He didn't lead me to the apartment building entrance as much as he dragged me.

"You don't have to see me to the door."

Maxim remained silent.

He rummaged in my purse for the keys and selected the correct outside door key on the first try. At first, I thought it was strange, then I remembered how he had been the one to change Dylan's locks earlier. Spikes of fear shot through me. I couldn't let him see me to my apartment door. I mean, besides being big and scary, he was literally carrying a black duffle bag. I watched true crime. I knew a murder bag when I saw one.

I stepped inside and turned around, blocking the entrance. "Thanks, but my *boyfriend* will be home and it's best he doesn't know about you," I lied.

He flipped up the hem of his shirt to show a handgun tucked into the waistband. "If I thought for a moment you weren't lying to me, there would be big trouble, babygirl."

When the fuck had he gotten a gun?

Duh, his car was probably full of them.

I swallowed as I stared at the gun. Letting this man drive me home had been a colossal mistake. Dammit, I was no better than the dumb bitch in horror movies who ran toward the creepy cabin in the woods. How could I have been so stupid? "Are you going to kill me?"

"Not tonight."

"That's not funny."

"Who's laughing?"

Despite the warmth of his hoodie, I shook.

Maxim stepped inside, gently moving me to the side before wrapping his arm around my lower back. "Come on, babygirl. It's been a long day and I'm tired."

He led me up the dark staircase. "Remind me to have a word with your landlord about the lights and security in your building."

"Sure," I squeaked out.

Sure, why not?

And don't forget to add eggs to the grocery list.

Seriously, what the fuck was happening?

One moment he was a super scary Russian thug and the next he was acting like a concerned boyfriend.

Fuck, I'd never needed a glass of wine so badly in my life. No, screw the wine. I needed the hard stuff.

When we reached my apartment door, he unlocked it and pushed it open. I stood still just on this side of the threshold.

His voice was a soft purr over my shoulder. "Carinna, step inside."

I stared into the dark and chilly interior of my apartment. I didn't have the luxury of having enough money to keep the heat on when I wasn't home. I shook my head. "I don't want to."

He pulled gently on one long curl. "You don't have a choice."

"Do you promise to leave if I go in?"

"No."

There was that word again. No. My heart was beating so fast, I thought it would pound out of my chest. I couldn't get enough oxygen into my lungs. My head spun at the thought of being locked inside my apartment with him. Even if I had wanted to, I don't think I could've taken a single step on my shaking knees.

A powerful arm wrapped around my waist. He lifted me

up against his chest and carried me the two steps over the threshold and closed the door. His body shifted against my back as he reached behind him to lock the door.

My knees buckled as everything went black.

CHAPTER 5

arinna

"Bayu-bayushki-bayu, Ne lozhisya na krayu!"

The darkness receded like the parting of a dense fog. I could hear someone singing in a soft baritone, but I couldn't make out the words.

"Pridet seren'kiy volchok, I ukhvatit za bochok."

I opened my eyes to find Maxim leaning over me, softly stroking my hair.

He smiled. *"Dobro pozhalovat' obranto malyshka. Ti poteryala soznaniye."*

My brow furrowed. Had I hit my head? I must have because I couldn't understand a word he was saying. I raised my hand to check my head. "Is there blood?"

Maxim grasped my wrist and drew my arm down. "Apologies, little one. I was speaking Russian. You have not hit your head. You only fainted, but I caught you before you hit the floor."

I fainted.

Fainted?

I shook my head but stopped when a spike of pain hit my right temple. "No. That's not possible. I've never fainted in my life."

Maxim shrugged, then winked. "I have that effect on women."

I scooted back into an upright position on my sofa. Then checked to make sure I was still wearing all my clothes. I was. Well, sort of. I still had his soccer hoodie on.

Maxim held out a juice glass that was filled with two fingers of liquid. "Here, drink this."

I gingerly took the glass from him. "What is it?"

"Tequila."

"Tequila?"

"It was all I could find that was remotely drinkable in your liquor cabinet. I've never met someone with cheaper taste in alcohol than my friend Vaska, but I think you may have him beat."

I sniffed at the glass contents, satisfied when I smelled the acrid citrus scent of tequila. "Well, not all of us can afford Patron." I kicked back the shot, breathing in as the fiery liquid hit my belly.

I handed him back the glass. "Another, please."

He rose and crossed the small space to the open kitchen. The moment he turned his back, I flew off the couch and searched the room quickly for some kind of weapon. As he turned back, I snatched the only thing near me. A selfie stick. I held the stick in front of me. "Don't come any closer."

Maxim drank the shot he had poured for me and reached casually for the liquor bottle as he leaned against the small kitchen island. "You are turning out to be far more amusing than I expected." He poured two more shots.

I gripped the selfie stick harder as I extended it as far as it would go. "Is this about Dylan and the money? She gave it back to your friend."

Maxim shook his head. "No. This is not about the money."

My eyes teared up. "Have you hurt Dylan? Where is she?"

She was supposed to be on a date with her soon to be ex-boyfriend Oliver, but I hadn't heard from her all night.

"Your friend is with my associate, Ivan."

"Ivan? The other Russian dude?"

"The same."

I had wrongfully encouraged Dylan to go out with Ivan instead of Oliver, but I thought she refused to listen to me. How could she be with Ivan?

"Is he going to hurt her?"

"Only if she asks for it."

"That's not funny."

"I'm not laughing."

My eyes moved between him and the bag he'd brought and back again.

Sensing my thoughts, he said, "It's only clothes."

"I don't believe you."

He nodded toward the bag. "See for yourself."

Keeping my gaze trained on him, I tipped the bag over, dumping the contents on the floor.

Maxim gestured toward the bag. "See? No duct tape, or ski mask, or zip ties. Just clothes."

So it wasn't a murder bag. That didn't mean he wasn't here to murder me.

"Why did you come to my work tonight?"

"Because I wanted to see you."

"How did you find out where I worked? Are you having me and Dylan followed?"

"It is easy tracking you American women down. You put your whole life on social media. That is something we will have to change, *moya malen'kaya iskra*. My little spark. You will have to delete your accounts. I can't have you posting such things for anyone to see."

I paced from one side of the room to the other, while keeping my selfie stick trained on him. "Oh, sure, I'll delete my accounts. No problem. And while I'm at it, how about I quit my job and start sewing my own dresses?"

He took several steps toward me. I backed up. He placed the juice glass with the shot of tequila on the table and backed away. "I am glad we are in agreement, although you will not have to sew your own clothes. I will be happy to provide you with clothes, jewels, whatever you need."

I grabbed the glass and drank the tequila, never needing a rough drink more. This was crazy. "Okay, for starters, that was sarcasm. I have absolutely no intention of deleting my social media accounts, or quitting my job, assuming I still have one after that stunt you pulled tonight, or accepting any clothes from you."

Maxim lifted his shirt and pulled out his handgun.

My heart stopped.

Even if I knew where my purse was, I wouldn't be able to reach it and get to my cell phone to call the police in time.

He clicked something on the gun and slid out the magazine. Then placed both pieces on the counter. "I believe I have given you the wrong impression. As I have said, this is not about your friend or the money. I tracked you down this evening because I wanted to see you again."

I ran my hand through my now hopelessly tangled hair. "You wanted to see me again? Why?"

Maxim rubbed his jaw as his heated gaze wandered down from my eyes, to linger at my mouth, then shifted lower.

My breath hitched. I had to look down at his hands to confirm he hadn't physically touched me. Finally, he spoke. "I thought you were cute. You are a little spark. Wait, no, how do they say it in America? A spitfire! You are quite a spitfire. I am in town for a few months. Perhaps we could have some fun."

Wait, he was trying to *date* me?

"In America, men usually strike up a conversation with you in the Starbucks line and then maybe ask for your phone number. They don't barge into your place of work and break a guy's nose!"

Maxim shrugged. "He's lucky I didn't slit his throat."

I frantically waved the selfie stick in his direction. "You see? That comment, right there? That's an *insane* thing to say. *You* are insane." I waved the selfie stick around me. "*All* of this is insane." Warming up to my rant, I continued, "In America, you don't force a woman into your car and then force your way into her apartment, even if you think she's cute. All of that is hella illegal!"

Still leaning against the island, Maxim spread his arms out. "And yet, here we are."

I swallowed as my cheeks heated. "And you definitely don't call her a *whore*."

His eyes narrowed. "You were dressed like one."

"That's not the point."

"Yes, it is. And it won't happen again. I won't be allowing you to dress like that in front of other men. Because if it does happen again, I guarantee you, any man that looks at you won't be leaving with just a broken nose."

I gestured with the selfie stick to the door. "No… *it won't happen again* because you are leaving right now."

"No."

"You don't have a choice. This is my apartment, and I'm ordering you to leave."

Maxim rose to his full height.

Holy hell, this man was trouble. Women probably threw their panties at him as he walked down the street. His face was all hard angles, from his slightly crooked nose that obviously had been broken at some point, probably from a fist fight, to the sharp line of his jaw. He was without a doubt the most sinfully handsome man I had ever laid eyes on. I was going straight to hell just for looking at him. He was like one of the bad boys from my Kindle romances. The kind you swooned over in a book but knew would be a disaster to date in real life. All the more reason to get him out of my apartment and out of my life.

He took several steps toward me. I raised the selfie stick in front of me as I backed away and tried to put a low upholstered chair between us. When he spoke, the hard edge had returned to his voice, deepening his accent. "It is you who does not have a choice here."

"I'll call the police."

"And when they arrive, they will see who I am, and they will leave."

He had said something similar at the bar. He didn't even seem fazed when I threatened to call the authorities. What kind of man wasn't afraid of the police? A rich one? Or perhaps a criminal. "Who are you?"

He bowed slightly. "Maxim Konatantinovich Miloslavsky, at your service. And you are Carinna Giovanna Russo. Born and raised in Chicago. Both parents are still living, although you've been on your own since you were in high school. You—"

"Stop! Stop! How do you know all this about me?"

"I have *connections* and I've told you… you interest me."

I tightened my grip on the selfie stick as I held it aloft before me. "Well, you don't interest me."

Maxim clucked his tongue as he took another step closer. "You are a terrible liar, *moya malen'kaya iskra*."

"Please, why won't you leave?"

Maxim circled around the chair.

I held the selfie stick up. "Stay back."

He grabbed the stick and tossed it aside. He then wrapped his arm around my waist and pulled me flush against his chest. He placed a hand around my neck and pressed up against my jaw, tilting my head back. "I'm not leaving, and if you were honest with yourself, you'd admit you don't want me to."

My lower lip trembled. "You frighten me."

He gently kissed my cheek, then my lips, then the tip of my nose. "Never be frightened of me, babygirl. I would never harm such a beautiful creature as you." He ran his tongue over my lower lip. "A beauty like yours is to be treasured, worshiped."

His mouth teased mine. I breathed in his air, falling deeper under his spell. My eyes half-closed as he lowered his head. At the last possible minute, sanity returned. I pushed him away. "No. I can't. This is too crazy. You have to leave."

Maxim rubbed his jaw. Then pierced me with a glare. "I knew it."

I surveyed him suspiciously. "Knew what?"

Without saying another word, he grabbed me by the back of the head and crushed his mouth to mine. He gave no quarter as his tongue speared inside my mouth, taking ownership. As I struggled in his grasp, he pulled up the hoodie from behind. A cool breeze touched my lower back before the first sharp sting of his slap. The impact drove my hips against his, where I felt the hard outline of his cock pressing against his jeans.

He spanked me again and again. His mouth swallowed my cries. With each heated slap, I was pushed against his hips.

He fisted my hair and deepened the kiss before finally breaking free. "This is what you want. Isn't it, babygirl? Not sweet words of love, but rough and dirty with a hint of pain."

The truth of his words struck at my very soul. Oh, God! "No, no! You're wrong!"

Using his grip on my hair, he pushed me facedown over the edge of the low chair. For the second time that night, he yanked down my leggings, exposing my ass. I braced, but wasn't prepared for the intense, humiliating pain of his palm striking my bare flesh. My pussy clenched as the stinging heat pooled between my legs.

He pulled my hair as he pressed his crotch against my ass, the rough denim sending sparks of pain across my tortured skin. He rubbed my right butt cheek, then squeezed it hard. I squealed in pain as I rose up on my toes.

"Tell me you like this," he commanded.

I buried my face in the back upholstery of the chair. The fabric muffled my response. "I don't. It hurts."

"That's the whole point, babygirl." His booted foot stepped on my leggings till they were around my ankles. He then kicked my legs wider. His hand moved in circles over my lower back under the hoodie to caress my ass before moving lower.

I panicked and tried to twist my legs closed.

He spanked my ass before moving his right hand between my legs.

I groaned, knowing what he would find.

His fingers teased my wet pussy.

Maxim leaned down and whispered in my ear. "My beautiful little liar. How shall I punish you for lying to me again?"

He pushed two fingers deep into me. Losing all inhibition, I groaned and arched my back.

Maxim sank his teeth into the side of my neck before licking the wound. "Such a greedy, tight little pussy," he teased as he thrust his fingers in and out in a torturously slow rhythm.

My mind shattered. All I could focus on was the twisted,

macabre dance of pleasure and pain he was leading me through. Every inch of my body hummed with awareness.

He continued to thrust his fingers inside of me as he rubbed his denim-covered, hard cock against my hip. I clawed at the fabric of the chair. The pressure kept building and building. My breath became labored. I was so close.

He pulled on my hair again. The sharp sting nearly sent me over the edge as I ground my hips against the back of the chair, desperately trying to put some pressure on my swollen clit. He ran his teeth over the whorl of my ear as he whispered darkly, "Are you my dirty girl?"

Oh, God! I was so close. At that point, I would have said yes to anything. "Yes! Yes! I'm your dirty girl," I breathed.

He pushed a third finger inside of me. My body strained to accommodate him. It had been so long.

"Tell me you want me to stay."

The pad of his thumb teased my asshole. My inner thighs clenched. "Please stay," I begged.

He pulled his fingers free. I immediately felt the loss. Pulling on my hair, he tilted my head all the way back. "Open your mouth."

I obeyed without question.

He pushed his three fingers past my lips. I tasted the undeniable proof of my arousal. He moved his fingers in deeper till my shoulders hunched as I gagged. "Take it. You'll have to learn to take every inch of me, babygirl." He pulled his fingers free, then forced them past my lips a second time. I choked and grabbed at his wrist as I shamelessly swirled my tongue around his fingers.

"Good girl," he purred.

I barely heard him. At that moment, I just wanted to come. "Please," I begged.

"No, you don't get to come just yet."

Dazed, I thought I heard him wrong. "What?"

CHAPTER 6

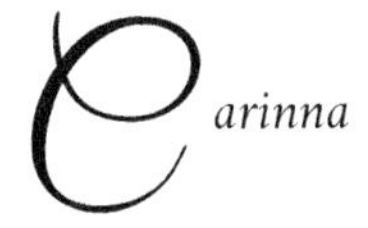*arinna*

He kicked my leggings aside and swooped me up into his arms. Carrying me across my small living room, he kicked open the bathroom door. He placed me on my feet and pulled open the shower curtain. He flicked on the tap, turning it all the way. Steam immediately rose. "First, I want you to wash off the looks of all those men."

He did not just say what I thought he said. My mouth opened in shock. "You… you… you…" I was so stunned all I could do was choke out a stuttered response.

He towered over me and placed a finger under my chin. "I think the word you are looking for is bastard."

"Bastard!"

He stroked my cheek. "You are so adorably stubborn. Don't pretend you haven't been longing for a nice hot shower. Are you going to deny yourself just to spite me?"

So now he was a mind reader too? Damn him.

"How do I know you're not just going to rob me blind while I'm in the shower?"

He ruffled my hair. "So cute. As if there was anything in this place to steal."

I placed my hands on my hips. "Hey!"

Sure, my apartment was small and filled with secondhand furniture. The TV didn't have cable and the refrigerator barely kept things cool, but it was clean and neat and all mine. It wasn't my fault my parents guilted me into giving them half my tips each week. Well, it was my fault, but there was no point in dwelling on the past. My brother was dead. I had killed him and now I needed to pay for that. If that meant not having a comfortable life filled with things like cable and a new sofa, then so be it. I would pay my penance, but that didn't mean I wanted it thrown in my face by Mr. Expensive Suit and Fancy Car. If my apartment was so tiny and below his standards, he could leave like I had already asked him to do a thousand times.

I hadn't been lying when I said he frightened me. The man scared the crap out of me in more ways than one. Sure, there were the obvious criminal overtones to everything he said and did, and his connection to the man who chased Dylan down to get back his hundreds of thousands of dollars in illegal cash. Then, of course, there were the super scary tattoos. Even the silver rings he wore on his fingers seemed to have a sinister edge to them. Like there was something uber-masculine about a man who said fuck what society thinks, I'm wearing jewelry.

Then of course there were his hands, his mouth, his... Damn, the man was the living embodiment of sex on a stick. Men like that were dangerous and scary as hell. Men like that held a power over women and they knew it. Big D energy was no joke. It had the power to convince a woman to do just about anything—like letting a man stay in her apartment while she showered.

He gestured over my head. "Shower," he said, before leaving the bathroom and closing the door behind him.

I raced over and pressed my ear to the door and listened, but couldn't hear anything. As the bathroom filled with steam, I paced in the confined space. Was I really just going to shower as if there wasn't a six-foot-five tattooed and pierced Russian criminal in my living room right now?

This was crazy.

This was insane.

This was bonkers!

Okay, my options. Option number one, I could catch him by surprise by racing out of the bathroom, through the apartment and out in the hall where I would scream bloody murder for the police. Option two, I could get a hot shower and then have what would probably be the best sex of my life.

Option one was definitely the sensible and sane option, but option two sounded way more fun. Hadn't I just told my best friend Dylan, only a few hours earlier, that she should go after the hot Russian guy who was the epitome of a bad boy romance hero come to life? Wouldn't I be a complete hypocrite if I didn't take my own advice?

This was crazy.

This was insane.

This was bonkers!

I wiped the steam off the mirror and stared at my reflection. Was I really going to do this? I looked over my shoulder at the shower, which was still running. Fuck it. I'd take a shower and then decide. I pulled the hoodie over my head. I started to fold it neatly with the intention of giving it back to Maxim, but then glanced over at the wicker hamper. I lifted the hoodie to my face and inhaled its spicy cologne scent.

Biting my lip, I went over to the hamper and lifted the lid. I placed the hoodie on top of the laundry before slipping off my thong and stepping into the shower.

I had to stifle a groan of relief when the hot water cascaded down my back. Damn him. He was right. I needed this. But after a few glorious minutes of standing under the shower stream, cold reality crashed down.

Shit! I needed to hurry. Grabbing my razor, I gave my legs a quick shave. I then scrubbed all the makeup off my face and lathered my hair. Finally, feeling more like a woman and less like a beer-drowned rat, I picked up my hot pink pouf and squeezed an obscene amount of creamy body wash onto it. I was lathering my arm when the doorknob for the bathroom turned.

Slipping the shower curtain aside, I poked my head out. "Oh, my God! What are you doing in here?"

Maxim stood in the center of my tiny bathroom. The moment he entered, all the air was sucked out of the room, leaving just a vacuum of dark sexual energy that pulsed all around him.

He had taken off his shirt and unbuttoned the top button on his jeans. Jesus, he just looked so damn dirty-sexy-wrong! With all those tattoos and piercings. And of course he would have rock-hard abs that led to a freaking Beckham.

He was holding the juice glass we'd shared. Before answering, he swallowed back another shot of tequila, then set the glass on the sink. "I'm joining you."

My eyes widened as I held my hot pink pouf protectively over my breasts. "The hell you are! Get out!"

Maxim kicked off his right boot, then his left. He then reached for the zipper of his jeans.

With a cry, I ducked my head back into the shower. Tilting my head back, I called out over the rush of water,

"Seriously, Maxim. Don't you dare come in here. You can shower after I'm done."

Letting a man as handsome as him see me naked in bed was one thing, but in the shower was an entirely different thing. In bed, I could arch my back and put my knee up and over my hip to make my thighs look sleeker than they really were. I could drape the sheet over my decently flat but not crazy-model-with-abs-flat belly. And all kinds of faults would be hidden by the dim light given off by my single lightbulb nightstand lamp with the red paisley scarf over the shade.

None of that was true in the damn shower!

I would just be standing here all wet and naked with no makeup on.

A rustle of fabric told me he had kicked off his jeans. Next, I saw a hand draw the curtain back. In a panic, I pushed on the curtain, trying to keep it closed. After a brief tug of war I was destined to lose, Maxim pulled the curtain all the way back and stepped into the shower with me.

His body was so big, his head was slightly above the curtain rod. I had to step back till my calf hit the tub faucet.

Maxim bit his lower lip as he surveyed me up and down. I tried to place an arm over my upper legs and one over my breasts, but he grabbed my wrists and stretched my arms out wide. "Goddamn, babygirl. You are one gorgeous piece of ass."

I wanted to object to the crude way he called me a piece of ass.

I wanted to.

I truly did.

The feminist in me cried out, then curled up into a fetal position for being objectified in such blunt terms.

The problem was it made my stomach take a delicious

flip and other parts of me tingle. I had to suppress a damn giggle. Fuck, this man was trouble.

Since he was taking his time appreciating my body, I figured turnabout was fair play. His chest was a violent art mural of bleeding hearts, guns, hammers and sickles, flames, and other Russian religious and propaganda symbols. The piercings only added to the sinister appeal of the macabre display. My gaze inched lower. I sucked in my lower lip as I followed the faint dusting of hair from his belly button to his… oh, my fucking God.

No.

Nope.

Hell to the no.

I blinked several times, still unable to trust my vision.

The man didn't have a penis. He had a damn battering ram.

And worse… I blinked again.

Yuupp.

He had a freaking reverse Prince Albert piercing.

CHAPTER 7

axim

I REALLY WAS A SICK BASTARD. I wrapped my hand around my almost painfully hard cock and stroked the length as I stared at Carinna. There was something about the fear and wonder reflected in her soft brown eyes that stirred my blood. I wanted her to be afraid. I wanted her to know it was going to hurt to fuck me. I wanted to taste her fear and relish every tremble and quake.

Like I said, I was a sick bastard.

Carinna shook her head as she stared at my cock. "Keep that *thing* away from me."

My lips lifted in a ghost of a smile. "No."

I knew she hated how often I said that word, but there was no fucking way I was staying away from this woman. She was turning out to be far more entertaining than I could have imagined. It was as if a halo of bright white sparks surrounded her, and those sparks burned brighter and brighter each time she opened that sassy mouth of hers or flashed me a defiant look. There was this driving need to harness that energy and make it my own. I needed to be inside of her. To feel her fire at the source.

Carinna turned and gripped the shower curtain as she prepared to leave. I snatched her warm, wet body from behind and pulled her close. A tremor ran down my limbs at the impact. It was just as I suspected. Finally holding her naked body was like holding a live wire.

My left hand reached across her chest and gripped her right breast, and my right arm extended low to cup her pussy. Leaning down, I licked the water off her neck. "You're not going anywhere."

With my foot, I flicked the knob to turn the water to its hottest temperature. I then turned our bodies to shelter her from the harsh pounding of hot water. The small bathroom chamber filled with fresh steam. It heated my lungs.

As her long tendrils of hair tickled my chest, I pinched her left nipple, relishing her shocked gasp.

Her breathing intensified. She was so responsive to my touch, it was like a drug. I'd barely gotten started and yet I could tell she was primed and ready to come.

She wrapped her small hand around my wrist. "Listen, I've... I've changed my mind."

Ignoring her, I traced the gentle seam of her pussy with a single fingertip.

She continued. "Seriously, I thought I was the type of girl who could throw caution to the wind and have a fun one-night stand, but I'm not. I'm not that girl. I can't do this."

It was cute she thought this was going to be a one and done, one-night stand. I hadn't even gotten my cock wet inside of her yet and I already knew once would not be enough. She was direct and honest. She spoke her mind without giving a damn about the consequences. After years of being surrounded by women who put on a thick facade of artifice, never saying a wrong word or acting out of turn, it was intoxicating. I didn't have to wonder how Carinna truly felt. She boldly told me. And I knew precisely how my every touch affected her because each emotion played out not only on her face but in the movements of her body. She was an open book and instead of finding that boring or less of a challenge, it fascinated me.

I pushed one finger inside her, knowing she'd still be wet from earlier.

She pulled on my wrist, trying to dislodge my hand. "Are you listening to me? I can't do this. We have to stop."

"No." Stopping was not an option. I truly felt I would go mad if I didn't get a chance to taste her, to feel her writhing beneath my weight as I thrust inside her delicious warmth.

"Stop saying that word."

I pushed a second finger inside. Fuck, she was tight. I circled the pad of my thumb over her clit, alternating the pressure with each stroke, building her up. Pressing my cock against her lower back, I ran my lips over the top of her shoulder as my left hand tested the heavy weight of her breast. "Then stop fighting me. This is happening, babygirl."

I pushed a third finger in.

She rose on her toes.

I thrust my fingers in deep, over and over again as the side of my thumb brushed her clit.

Her head fell back against my shoulder. "Oh… oh… oh…"

Now she wasn't grasping my wrist to pull it away, but rather to hold it in place as her hips rocked against the palm of my hand.

"That's it, *moya malen'kaya iskra*. Come for me."

Her ass clenched as her hips thrust forward against my hand. I couldn't wait to get her bent over the bed with a leather strap in my hand. The next time I felt her ass against my cock, I wanted it to be on fire from a punishment strapping.

Releasing my grasp on her breast, I gripped her long, wet hair. I yanked her head back and growled into her ear. "The moment you come, I'm dragging you out of this shower and wrecking this tight pussy of yours with my cock."

I could feel the vibration of her moan against my lips as I kissed just beneath her ear.

"I'm going to bend you over that bed and fuck you so hard you forget your own name."

Her body jerked within my grasp. She was close. I could feel it.

"I'm going to make my dirty girl fall to her knees and lick every drop of come off my cock." I bit her earlobe. "Would you like that, baby? You want to be my little whore?"

"Oh, God," she moaned as her thighs clenched around my hand.

I wrapped my fist around her hair and pulled tighter. Her body bowed as I thrust my fingers in harder. "You want me to pound into you until you scream for mercy?"

Carinna reached up her arm and grabbed my hair as her other hand fondled her own breast.

Goddamn, this woman was fucking hot as hell.

"Don't stop," she breathed.

Our bodies rocked together with the rhythm of my fist, as I twisted my three fingers into her cunt as far as they would go. "Tell me you want to fuck me. Tell me you want me to treat you like the dirty girl you are and fuck this sweet pussy raw," I demanded.

Her body bucked in my arms as she came. "Yes! God, yes! Fuck!"

I tore at the shower curtain so fiercely it ripped off the rod.

Sweeping her into my arms, I carried her out of the bathroom and into the bedroom.

CHAPTER 8

Maxim

I DROPPED her onto the center of the bed and climbed up after her. Her wet skin glistened in the faint light. Wrapping my hands around her thighs, I pulled her closer. "You look good enough to eat."

She was out of breath when she protested, "I just came. I'm too sensitive."

I placed her knees on my shoulders and grasped her ass. "We'll see about that. I want to hear you scream my name this time."

I flicked my tongue along her seam, then pushed it in deeper. The tip circled around her swollen clit. "Damn, you taste good, baby."

Carinna groaned as she fisted the bedcover.

I swished my tongue from side to side, playing with her clit as my hands squeezed her ass, knowing she'd still be sore from the spanking I'd given her earlier. The first of many.

"Play with your tits," I growled against her pussy.

Carinna obeyed, placing her palms over both breasts as I teased and tortured her clit. It wasn't long before she came a second time. "Oh, God! Oh God!"

The moment she did, I flipped her onto her stomach and wrenched her up onto her knees. Raising my arm, I brought my open palm down on her ass cheek so hard she pitched forward. "I thought I told you I wanted to hear you scream my name when you came."

I wrenched her back onto her knees and spanked her ass again.

"I'm sorry!" she squealed. "I'm sorry!"

I grasped her hair and pulled it hard. "Not good enough."

With my fist in her hair, I spanked her ass several more times until the heat of her skin permeated my palm. Her pale flesh glowed a hot cherry red by the time I was done. I couldn't wait to feel the heat of it against my balls as I fucked her deep. "Spread your knees."

When she didn't obey fast enough, I used my own to open hers wide as I pushed her face into the covers. Grasping my cock, I wet the head at her entrance, using the steel ball of my piercing to once again tease her clit.

Carinna pitched forward a second time. She scrambled a few feet away and gripped the headboard. "Wait. Condom. You need a condom."

I grabbed her hips and forced her back into position. "Are you clean?"

"Yes, of course. It's been ages, but I've never done it without a condom."

That's all I needed to hear. "Fuck a condom."

Never in my life had I said those words, but there was just something about this woman. A condom implied this was just another fucking. That she was just another pussy. I already knew that wasn't the case. She was different, and I wouldn't tolerate anything between us. I needed to feel every glorious inch of her as I thrust in deep.

I eased the head in, careful not to tear her. Once I felt her body close around the tip, I placed my hands on her hips and thrust to the hilt. Carinna cried out as her body absorbed the full impact. "Maxim!"

I growled through my teeth as her tight pussy clenched around my cock.

And that was my last sane moment.

After that, I became a man possessed. I relentlessly pounded into her, as if my very life depended on it. I couldn't get enough of her hot, wet cunt as I thrust in repeatedly. Looking down between us, I saw my shaft wet with her arousal before it would impale deeply into her body. Her ass bore my handprints as I gripped her hips and anchored her to take each forceful thrust.

Releasing her hip, I fisted her hair and pulled her upright on her knees. With my free hand, I pinched her nipples, hard. "That's it, dirty girl. Take that cock. Take it deep."

Carinna moaned.

I moved my hand from her breasts to her pussy. I slapped it hard.

"Ow!" whimpered Carinna.

From this angle, I was thrusting in even deeper, impaling her upright body straight down on my cock. "Say my name."

"Maxim," she said on a weak exhale as her head fell back onto my shoulder.

"Louder," I yelled.

"Maxim!" she screamed as her pussy clamped down on my cock, the ripples of her third orgasm crashing up my shaft.

Right before I came, I pulled free. Using my grip on her hair, I maneuvered her onto her knees before me. "Open your mouth."

Her gaze pleaded with me as she kept her lips closed.

I shook her head, fisting her hair tighter. I clamped my free hand around her jaw. "I said, open your mouth, whore." I pushed my fingers into her cheeks, forcing her mouth open.

I pushed my cock past her lips. "Say my name."

She obeyed, trying to speak past my thick shaft shoved down her throat.

"Again," I demanded, loving the vibrations it sent up my cock. I could hear the clatter of my piercing against the back of her teeth.

My name was on her lips when I came, coating her tongue with my seed.

I lifted her upright by her hair till our bodies were flush together in the center of the bed. I pushed a glob of semen, which had drizzled past the corner of her mouth, to her lips. I then forced two fingers into her mouth. "Suck them as you swallow my come."

She sucked them. Spearing her tongue between my fingers, then swirling it about.

"Suck them clean."

The moment she finished, I wrapped my hand around her throat and tilted her head back. "You liked that, didn't you? You enjoyed being treated like my dirty little whore."

Her eyes filled with tears. "Don't make me say it."

My free hand caressed down her back. I pushed my fingers between her ass crack to tease her tight, puckered hole. "Admit it or I'll prove it to you another way."

Her eyes widened. "Don't. I've never."

I chuckled. "Oh, trust me, babygirl. Your pert ass is going to have a pretty little gape by the time I'm done ravaging it. It's your choice whether you want me to turn you over and fuck you raw right this moment."

She blurted out, "I admit it! All right. I admit it. I like how you… how you… *used* me."

"That's my good girl." I released her and climbed off the bed. I padded naked into the bathroom and wet a small hand towel under the shower stream that we had left running. Flipping the nozzle off, I returned to the bedroom.

Carinna was standing next to the bed, reaching into a bureau drawer and pulling out a T-shirt.

I frowned. "What do you think you're doing?"

"Just getting a shirt."

I motioned toward the bed. "Get your ass back on that bed before I spank it black and blue. Now!" I growled.

With a small yelp, she scrambled to obey.

"Now lie back and spread your legs."

Her thighs trembled as she struggled to obey me.

I climbed back onto the bed and kneeled between her open thighs. I placed the warm hand towel over what I knew had to be her sore pussy. Once I had wiped the evidence of our lovemaking from her, I returned to the bathroom to toss the towel into the hamper. I pushed aside a pair of yoga pants and lifted up the sleeve of my hoodie. Smiling at the thought of her wanting to keep it. I liked the idea of her cute little body snuggling up in my sweatshirt.

When I returned to the bedroom, it was dark. Her slight form was already curled up under the covers.

I crossed to the bed and lifted the blanket.

Carinna rose on one elbow and looked over her shoulder at me. "What are you doing?"

"I'm going to bed."

"You mean you're staying? You're not leaving? But… but we're done."

I wrapped my arm around her waist and pulled her close. Her backside cradled my cock. Nudging her partially dry hair aside, I whispered into her ear, "Oh, *moya malen'kaya iskra*, I'm not even close to being done with you."

CHAPTER 9

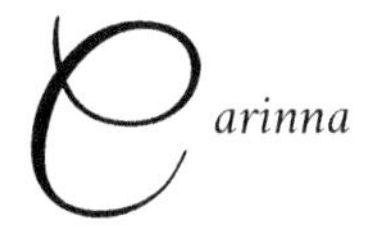

arinna

THE BED WAS empty when I woke up.

I reached my hand under the covers to feel the sheets where Maxim had slept.

They were cold.

Bringing my knees up to my chest, I huddled deeper under the blanket, feeling empty and alone and not sure why.

I shouldn't be surprised. I'd assumed he would leave the moment he got his rocks off. The fact that he stayed a few extra hours to get some sleep shouldn't be that big of a deal.

Except that it was a big deal.

In the past, I'd always avoided sleeping next to a guy. I hated how in romance novels the heroine would fall asleep like some freaking woodland creature curled up on a pillow of rose petals. Her hair was in smooth curls about her like a halo. Her cherry lips only gently parted as the back of her hand rested against her pale cheek. Her breathing was like the flapping of a butterfly's wings. The perfect sleeping beauty.

Problem was that so was not reality.

In reality, I was deathly afraid I'd kick the guy as I tossed and turned and stole the covers. Each morning my hair was a tangled mass of curls that any bird would envy for a nest and, to top it off, I was pretty sure I snored. All of that led to an anxiety-riddled night with little to no sleep. Because of that, I rarely let a guy sleep over. Not even a boyfriend on the rare occasion I ever had one.

I was certain I wouldn't sleep a wink with a man like Maxim in my bed. I mean he was like a towering inferno of lust and sexual threats. He practically hummed with criminal stay-the-fuck-away-from-me energy. The sound of the red flags flapping around his head alone should have kept me awake. And yet it didn't.

The moment his powerful arm closed around my waist and pulled me close, I was sound asleep in his embrace. The entire night was just a cozy memory of feeling warm and protected—which was, of course, insane. No one in their right mind would feel warm and safe around Maxim.

I mean, the man had pulled my hair, smacked my ass, and called me a whore.

So why, in the name of all that was holy, had I actually liked it?

My cheeks burned at the memory of how I had let him talk to me.

That's it, dirty girl. Take that cock. Take it deep.

I'd never thought in a million years I'd be the 'spank my ass and call me pretty' kind of girl. Although, to be fair, only a man like Maxim could pull off that vibe. If any of the few men I had been with in the past had tried something like that, I would have laughed in their faces.

But not with Maxim.

I couldn't imagine ever laughing in that man's face.

He was just too intimidating, too strong, too big, too dangerous... too everything.

Last night was the absolute best sex of my life. It was raw and dirty and primal. It had none of the usual awkward niceties I'd have expected from a first-time encounter. I'd never had a one-night stand before, but usually the first time with a new boyfriend was always more of a specially choreographed event. Typically, I'd buy some new sexy lingerie. I'd make sure the bedroom had flattering lighting and clean sheets that smelled of fabric softener and perfume. Alcohol would definitely be involved. And of course, newly researched sex positions from a *Cosmo* article, so I'd come across as *adventurous and fun* in bed.

That was not the case last night.

Instead of a glass of wine with an elegant dinner, I got a few trauma tequila shots and a slap on the ass before he fucked me sideways. I'm pretty sure Maxim would have no patience for lingerie either. I had this image of him shredding an expensive Victoria's Secret thong because it got in his way.

And oh, my God, the Prince Albert piercing!

I had actually felt the metal ring and ball rub along the inside of my pussy with each thrust. And the way he used it to tease my clit? Jesus, I was getting wet all over again just thinking about it. When he pushed his cock into my mouth, I was certain it was going to crack my front teeth, but in that moment, I hadn't given a damn. The sex was that good.

I rubbed my eyes and cheeks. Thank goodness he had left quietly while I was still sleeping. I didn't think I could have faced him in the stark bright light of morning.

Dark deeds needed to stay in the darkness where they freaking belonged.

And so did insanely dangerous and stupid one-night

stands. Not only was Maxim definitely not boyfriend material, he was way too intense to even be a friend with benefits fuck. Seriously, that man needed to return to the wilds of Russia, and soon. A man like him shouldn't be wandering around polite society with so many unsuspecting and vulnerable women about.

I reached over to my nightstand for my phone to text Dylan before realizing it was still in my purse in the living room. The battery probably died ages ago. I would have to call her the moment I had my coffee and find out how her date went with Oliver. And to find out if what Maxim said last night was true. Had she eventually met up with Ivan as well? I couldn't wait to find out.

How was I ever going to explain my crazy one-night stand to her? I wasn't even sure I understood my own actions. Perhaps another person's perspective was just what I needed.

Once again, my hand moved over the cold sheet.

Was it weird that I missed him? Of course it was! I barely knew the man and in the few hours we'd spent together, we had spent half of them fighting and the other half fucking. That was hardly the basis for an ongoing relationship, not that he was offering… or that I was accepting!

Stop it.

This was a one and done quick one-night stand outrageous fling. That was all.

I would file it away as a fond memory of that time I did something crazy and stupid and dangerous and fun.

I stretched and cringed as my sore thighs complained.

Holy hell, had it been fun.

As I rolled over and tucked the blanket higher over my shoulder, the dark rich smell of coffee reached my nose. I smiled. Dylan. She must have used her key to bring me coffee. Since I had a pastry class later this morning, she would have assumed I was already up. She was probably waiting in the living room to tell me all about her boring date with Oliver. Hopefully, her story ended with some juicy details about Ivan, although I doubt her time with Ivan would compete with my time with Maxim.

I slipped out of bed and reached into my bureau to grab a T-shirt. I bit my lip and glanced over my shoulder at the bathroom door. I crossed the threshold and dug Maxim's hoodie out of the hamper. I sniffed it. It still smelled like his cologne. I pulled it over my head. Sure, I was being silly and maybe even sentimental, but it wasn't like he would know!

After swishing some mint mouthwash to get the taste of tequila… and other things… out of my mouth, I walked out of the bedroom and into the kitchen.

Leaning against the kitchen island, impeccably dressed in a pair of slate gray slacks and a pale violet dress shirt, was Maxim.

CHAPTER 10

arinna

He opened one of my kitchen cabinets and pulled out one of my favorite, if chipped, mugs. It was a gift from Dylan. It had a bright blue baking mixer on it and said *Certified Bad Ass Baker*. And it looked absolutely ridiculous in his massive, masculine, completely inked-up hands. For half a second, I was worried he'd accidentally crush the thick porcelain to dust in his firm grasp. The memory of those same hands wrapped around my hair and pulling while he pounded into me from behind had my cheeks heating in humiliation all over again.

Turning, he lifted the pot out of the coffeemaker. "Good morning, *moya derzkaya devushka*. Coffee?"

Ders Kaya Dia Kush ka. I wondered what that meant? I would have to Google it later because I would be damned if I asked him. It probably meant something entirely unromantic in Russian, like *a piece of ass*.

What was he still doing here, anyway? I glanced around the kitchen. There were several white plastic grocery bags only half unpacked.

In the center of the island was my pink business plan binder. It was where I kept all of my recipes, notes, and research, as well as my draft business plan, hopefully to open my own pastry shop one day. It was clear he had been reading it.

Reaching over, I snapped the binder shut and cradled it to my chest. "What are you doing here?"

Maxim nodded toward my binder. "Your market research is sound, but your numbers are off. You need to factor in at least twelve percent cost for labor, not eight percent, and raise your product costs by five percent. I also think your profit forecasting for year two is too low."

I gripped the binder tighter as I jutted out my chin. "What the hell do you know about the bakery business? You're a—you're a—" Fuck. I didn't even know what he did for a living.

Maxim paused in raising a mug of coffee to his mouth. Staring at me over the edge of the mug, one eyebrow lifted. "An arms dealer?"

"An arms dealer!" I huffed indignantly. "Wait. What? You're a—a—" Dammit, my brain was not functioning right now. It had completely short-circuited the moment I saw him casually standing in my kitchen.

Maxim finished for me. "An arms dealer. Yes."

I shook my head. "Who just blurts out something like that?"

Maxim shrugged. "Someone who isn't ashamed of what they do for a living. Actually, my associates take care of the arms. I'm more of the numbers guy and deal facilitator."

I blinked. "You're a criminal!"

Maxim put down his coffee. "One man's crime is another's business opportunity." He circled around the island toward me.

I backed away. "You're a criminal!"

He wrenched the binder from my death grip and tossed it back onto the counter. "I'm going to need you to stop saying that so loudly. This shoebox you call an apartment has very thin walls."

My eyes widened as he backed me against the kitchen sink. "You're right. I should be calling for the police. Police! Police!"

I was screaming like an unhinged crazy person, but I couldn't help it. I had slept with an international arms dealer criminal last night… and we didn't use a condom. I could be carrying an international arms dealer criminal's baby right now. Okay, maybe not since I was on birth control, but still! My brain went from short-circuited to full meltdown.

Maxim placed a hand on either side of my hips as he leaned down, pinning me in place with his intense stare. "And I'm *definitely* going to need you to stop saying that."

I opened my mouth to scream again.

Before I could do so, his mouth claimed mine. It was a passionate no-holds-barred kiss. Although he was dressed in a suit, he hadn't shaved. The scruff of his five o'clock shadow scraped my cheek and jaw as his lips bruised mine. His tongue swept in to duel with my own. He tasted like coffee and sweet cream. His hand crept around my throat to cup the back of my neck as his thumb caressed my jawline. The hard press of his cock against my stomach was both a turn-on and a threat.

He broke our kiss and touched his forehead to mine. "You really are adorably beautiful when you first wake up."

He was lying. My hair was a riotous tangle of curls since I'd let it air dry as I slept. I had no makeup on, and I was wearing his wrinkled hoodie that I had fished out of my hamper. I glanced down. *Fuck, I'm wearing his hoodie.* Maybe I'd get lucky and he wouldn't notice I was wearing his clothing like some lovesick schoolgirl with a crush.

Maxim stroked my cheek. "Yes, I noticed, and yes, I like it."

My cheeks burned as a delicious warmth spread through my belly. Damn him. I reached down to pull it off, not caring that I was naked under it. I'd do the run of shame back to my bedroom rather than let him have the satisfaction.

His tattooed hands with several heavy silver rings on them stilled mine. His emerald gaze hardened. "Don't you dare take it off."

I inhaled a shaky breath as I fisted the soft material of the hoodie between my hands. "What now?"

"Now? I make you a cup of coffee." He moved away to open the cabinet and pull down another mug. He poured me a cup. "How do you take it?"

I averted my gaze, feeling uncharacteristically shy. "Cream and sugar, please."

He lifted the lid off my sugar bowl and spooned a teaspoon of sugar into the dark brew. He then looked up at me expectantly.

"More."

He spooned another teaspoon.

"More."

He raised an eyebrow and chuckled as he spooned a third overflowing teaspoon. He then turned to open the refrigerator.

I moved to open the cabinet over the coffeemaker. "It's not in there. It's in here." I pulled down the cheap powdered cream I used because I couldn't afford to always be buying the more expensive heavy cream.

Maxim furrowed his brow as his mouth twisted into a grimace. "No. I don't think so." He opened the refrigerator and pulled out a fresh carton of heavy cream. And a brand-name one no less, not a nameless store brand, one that I would usually buy when I indulged.

I stepped closer and peered into my refrigerator. It was filled with groceries. Eggs, bacon, milk, wedges of expensive cheese, beets, red cabbage, carrots, grapes, and apples. There was even a raw chicken and some red meat. I turned to face Maxim, who was calmly stirring the coffee he was preparing for me. "You went grocery shopping?"

"All I found in your refrigerator was a few half empty Chinese take away containers and a stack of something terrible-looking called *Lean Cuisine*. That is not food. We need to eat."

We?

Ignoring the cup of coffee he slid across the counter to me, I said, "*We* don't need to eat. *I* need to eat, and *you* need to eat, but there is no *we* need to eat." Great, now he had me sounding like a demented Dr. Seuss. A few more minutes in this man's presence and I'd be in a straitjacket eating my meals with a plastic safety spoon.

Maxim was unfazed. "Fine. We will dine out or order take away."

I cupped the mug between my hands and inhaled the rich scent. "It's called takeout in America," I grumbled before taking a sip. It was delicious. Too delicious. I glanced to my left at the coffee grounds bag on the counter. It was freshly ground coffee from the frou-frou expensive grocery store around the corner, not the stale pre-ground cheap crap I usually purchased. No wonder it was so heavenly. Damn him, again.

Before I could argue with him further, I glanced at the microwave clock. "Fuck! Is that the time? I have to go. I'm going to be late for class." I put the coffee mug down on the counter and ran toward my bedroom, tossing over my shoulder, "You can show yourself out."

It was a ballsy move ordering an international arms dealer criminal out of my apartment, but I didn't really know the rules for how to handle a one-night stand who hung around for coffee the next morning, let alone a big scary Russian one-night stand.

I raced over to my bureau and grabbed a pair of yoga pants and a tank top. I then rushed over to my bathroom. I closed and locked the door, just in case. After washing my face and brushing my teeth, I put on some makeup and piled my hair into a messy top-knot bun. I'd force it into a chef cap when I got to school. I grabbed a freshly pressed chef's coat from my closet and my sneakers before heading out of my bedroom.

Where I collided with Maxim.

Hopping on one foot, I slipped one sneaker on then the next. "Seriously, don't you have some supervillain criminal things to do?"

Maxim steadied me by my shoulders. His gaze wandered from my face to my chest and back. "You are not wearing that."

Shrugging him off, I tossed my chef coat over the back of my living room chair and searched for my purse. "What?" After finding my purse, I rummaged through and groaned when I found my cell phone. It barely had any battery juice left. No time to charge it. I grabbed my car keys before remembering that I wasn't the one who drove my car home last night. I rushed over to the front window and looked out on the street, then breathed a sigh of relief when I saw Lucy parked out front. From my vantage point, she didn't look like she had any broken windows. Maxim's henchman must have used a wire hanger to open it and then hot-wired it. Turning back to look at Maxim, I asked, "Hot wiring a car doesn't mess with the ignition, does it? Because I don't have time for that today."

He crossed his arms over his chest. Scowling at me from across the room, he ignored my question and said, "Go back in your room and change."

I shoved my *Baking and Pastry: Mastering the Art and Craft* textbook into my backpack along with my knife roll, which contained my pastry knives, spatulas, cutters, and thermometers. "What? Why? This is what I always wear to class." I looked down at my outfit. The tank top was a little snug, but it was nothing worse than you would see any other woman wearing to a gym or out shopping. Besides, I was going to put a chef jacket on over it as soon as I got to school.

Maxim stormed across the room and ripped the backpack from my hands. "Not anymore, you fucking don't. Now go and change," he commanded as he raised his arm and pointed to my bedroom door.

I reached to snatch my backpack from his grasp. He raised it higher over my head. With a frustrated sigh, I placed my fists on my hips. "Listen, last night was fun, but you're not my father or my boyfriend. You don't get to dictate to me what I can and can't wear!" Not like I'd let my father or a boyfriend do that either, but that was beside the point. First my corset top last night and now this. Who did this guy think he was?

I realized my mistake the moment I made it.

Maxim's entire body stiffened. His eyes narrowed as his nostrils flared. Tossing my backpack on the floor, he stalked toward me. I couldn't get away fast enough. His hand reached out to encircle my throat. He didn't squeeze; it was just enough pressure to control my movements. He forced me to walk backward till my body slammed into the wall behind me. He moved his hand to place his forearms on the wall over my head, caging me in.

All the air left the room. I kept breathing fast, but I wasn't taking any oxygen into my lungs. Like I was drowning on empty air.

Several agonizing seconds passed. His gaze moved slowly over my face and mouth, then lower. He moved one hand down to trace the low-cut neckline of my tank top with his fingertips. His touch was like a brand on my skin.

When he finally spoke, his tone was soft and deceptively polite. "I need to apologize. This is my fault. Apparently, I haven't made myself clear. I like you. So I'm going to keep you. For now. Which means you are mine."

He traced the outline of one nipple through the thin fabric of my tank top. He then pinched it hard.

I cried out and tried to rise on my toes. The pain was disturbingly erotic.

He leaned down and pressed his lips to mine to silence my cries before continuing, his voice a harsh whisper against my mouth. "I don't share what is mine *with anyone*. Any man looks at you, I kill him. It's that simple. So I will ask you one last time—politely—to go and change. If I have to ask you again, I won't be so polite. And I guarantee you won't be going anywhere if I do, because I will strip you bare and tie you to the bed till you learn to behave. Do we understand one another, babygirl?"

I swallowed. I opened my mouth several times to speak but couldn't force the words out past my fear. Finally, I just nodded my assent.

Maxim smiled, the gesture transforming the harsh angles of his face. Once again, he was the charming, laid-back guy who just made me coffee and bought me groceries. He playfully pulled on a curl that had fallen out of my loose bun. "Good girl. Now hurry up or you will be late for class. I will drive you."

Again, I could only nod. In a daze, I ducked under his arm

and returned to my bedroom. Unsure what to wear, I changed into a loose pair of straight leg yoga pants and a black long-sleeved T-shirt. For good measure, I wrapped a pale pink scarf around my throat so that it dangled over my breasts.

I emerged from the bedroom to see Maxim standing near the door. He had put on his suit jacket and was holding my backpack, purse, and chef's coat. "Come, *moya malen'kaya iskra*."

I still hadn't asked him what that meant, but now I suspected it meant something scary possessive. I couldn't see any way around it. I put on my jacket and followed him out of the apartment. He lifted my keys and locked the door, but instead of placing them back in my purse, he pocketed them. When he saw my curious look, he only winked and placed a hand on my lower back to escort me down the hallway.

We passed Dylan's door. I couldn't hear the usual blast of her TV, so she'd probably already left for work. Not that I would have involved her in this mess, anyway. I would let Maxim take me to school and then after class I would hide out at a friend's house or maybe scrape together some money for a hotel room near the airport.

One thing was certain: I was going to get as far away from this man as I possibly could.

CHAPTER 11

axim

I OPENED the passenger door for Carinna, then placed her belongings in the back seat. Circling around the back of the car, I hopped into the driver's seat and pulled away from the curb. I glanced to my right to see her sitting with her arms crossed over her chest and her lower lip protruding in a pout. She looked adorable when she was angry, not that now was the time to tell her that.

I had spoken to her harshly, which hadn't been my intention, but when she came out of that bedroom with her curves on full display in those tight yoga pants and her tits hanging out of that tiny tank top, I saw red.

If I were honest, my angry reaction had surprised even myself.

I'd had women in the past who dressed in far less as they paraded around in front of me and my friends. I couldn't recall ever giving a damn. In fact, I enjoyed the envious looks

I received from my friends, knowing I was the one who'd be fucking them later. What did I care if a woman had on a skirt that barely covered her ass and a see-through blouse with a barely there lace bra?

Yet, with Carinna, it was different.

Last night, walking into that bar and catching sight of her serving those men in that leather corset nearly drove me insane. It was all I could do not to pour vodka on the bar and set the place on fire with all those leering men trapped inside. I barely knew the woman, and yet somehow it was like they were touching what was mine.

Now, after tasting and sinking deep into that sweet pussy, I had even less restraint when it came to another man even glancing in her direction. For as long as I stayed in America, she was just going to abide by my rules or accept the consequences. I wouldn't hesitate to punish her and kill any man who got close to her.

I stopped at a light and reached over to her.

She started.

Not exactly the reaction I wanted.

Raising an eyebrow, I reached for the seat belt and stretched it over her chest and latched it before returning my attention to the cars in front of me. I gripped the steering wheel. She should be grateful I was letting her out of her apartment at all. Instead, I should have insisted she stay in bed naked, waiting for my return.

I smirked, warming up to the idea. Perhaps after today, I would insist she drop out of school for the rest of the semester and cater only to my needs. I would pay her handsomely for her full attention. After all, she couldn't have that much money, judging by the size and location of her apartment.

Thinking of her tiny place reminded me I needed to get the locks changed, just as with her friend Dylan. I would also have a word with her landlord regarding the lights and current security of the building. By the end of the day, only the Kremlin would be better guarded. While I was at it, I would order a larger bed. That simple double bed would not do for the both of us and what I intended to do to her curvy little body over the next few months. I would need something with a sturdier frame. Something with bedposts I could tie things to.

Driving on in silence, we finally pulled up to the community college where she took her pastry classes. As much as I planned on having her drop out for the next few months, her ambition was admirable. Perhaps, if she was a good girl, I would help her set up a cute little pastry shop, just like in her business plan. I had an obscene amount of money and rarely spent it on anything but myself. It would be nice to spend it making someone else happy for a change. I suddenly had a desire to see her pretty face light up in an appreciative smile when she learned of my generosity.

Plus, it would help solidify my control over her for when I returned to America. Ivan and I were increasing our business connections to Vaska and Dimitri's enterprise. I would travel to Chicago frequently over the next few years. It would be useful to have a warm and willing body waiting for me each time I returned. I could set her up in a home, and her little business would keep her occupied and out of trouble while I was gone.

Before the car had even come to a complete stop, Carinna had unlocked her belt and was trying to open the door. I engaged the automatic locks.

She kept her face averted as she tried the locked handle several times. "Thanks for the ride, but I have to go. I'm late."

It looked like my cute little plaything was going to still be stubborn about our new arrangement. It would be prudent to wait and tell her of my plans for her future. Right now, I needed to make sure she understood the rules. “Carinna, look at me.”

She didn’t turn but kept facing the passenger window. She tried the door handle again. This time more violently. “Seriously, I need to go. I’m late.”

I twisted in my seat and rested my forearm on the steering wheel. “Make me wait one second more and you will not be going at all.”

With a gasp, she turned to face me.

“That is better. What time are you finished?”

“I’ll just catch a ride home with a friend or take the Metra.”

“That’s not what I asked.”

“I don’t need a ride home from you.”

I reached for her chin and tilted her head back, capturing her gaze with mine. “What. Time. Are. You. Finished?”

Undaunted, her eyes narrowed as she matched my stare. “Why. Are. You. Asking?”

It was difficult keeping a straight face. Finding a woman with so much fire and sass was rare indeed, but finding one willing to try to stare me down was damn near impossible. She really was a unique find, one I had no intention of letting go.

I released her chin. “Fine. Have it your way.” I turned to open my car door.

“Wait! What are you doing?”

“Obviously, I’m going to attend class with you. I’ll just cancel my morning meetings.”

She blinked several times. I was fast learning. That was a cute tic of hers whenever she was taken aback by something I said or did. It was fascinating to see her collect her thoughts and regroup. Like an adorable kitten scratching the dirt and getting her tiny claws out, ready to attack. “The hell you are.

I'm not letting you follow me around like some goon bodyguard all day."

"Then I guess it is a good thing I wasn't planning on asking your permission. So what will it be, babygirl? Are you going to let me know when you are finished so I can drive you home, or do we spend the day together?"

Her knee bounced up and down in her agitation. "Fine! My classes are done at four."

I raised an eyebrow.

She bit her lip, then sighed. "Two-thirty."

I stroked her cheek, choosing to ignore it when she turned her face away. "Do I have to tell you what will happen if you are not here at two-thirty-five waiting for me?"

"No," she whispered.

"Good girl."

I unlocked the doors.

Carinna sprang out and before I could assist her, she had opened the back door and grabbed her belongings and sprinted up the cement stairs leading to the entrance. I waited till she was inside and the door was closing behind her before I pulled away.

Glancing at my dashboard, I realized I, too, was going to be late for my morning meeting. I smiled. Carinna was worth it.

* * *

I PULLED up to Red Star and tossed my keys to the valet. Opening the glass entrance door, I sprinted up the few stairs and gave a wink to the girl behind the counter to my left before heading down a second set of stairs straight into the men's locker room.

I accepted the large white robe, *shapka*, and towel handed to me by the attendant. "Have the others arrived?"

The older man shook his head while keeping his eyes averted. "No, sir."

I had learned from Ivan that this bathhouse was a favorite haunt of Vaska and Dimitri. It was a small taste of home in America. It wasn't unusual for them to rent out the entire space to have a meeting in private.

Removing my suit, I wrapped a towel low around my hips and headed into the *banya* space. A wave of one-hundred-sixty-degree heat from the stone oven to the left of the door hit me in the face. Making sure to shut the door behind me quickly, trapping the heat, I made my way in the darkened room to one of the stacked red cedar benches. I leaned back and stretched out my arms and enjoyed the hot, wet heat as it relaxed my muscles. Placing the oatmeal-colored felt *shapka* on my head, I let out a sigh of relief and closed my eyes.

A few minutes later, there was a waft of cold air as the door opened. I lifted one eyelid to see Vaska and Dimitri strolling in.

Vaska slapped me on the shoulder as he took a seat on the bench near me. "Maxim Kostya, *priyatno videt' tebya, moy drug.*"

"I tebya tozhe, Vaska. Ty khorosho vyglyadish', moy drug," I greeted him in return.

"Lyubov' khoroshey zhenshchiny, moy drug. Lyubov' khoroshey zhenshchiny!"

I leaned my head back and closed my eyes again. Of course, he would say the love of a good woman was the reason why he was looking so well. Ivan had told me about his meeting with Dimitri yesterday. The man was like a domesticated dog now, happily staying by his woman's fire. It was no surprise Vaska was the same way.

Without opening my eyes, I laughed. "Ivan was right. America has made you both soft."

Vaska gripped his cock through his towel. “That is not what my Mary would say.”

We all laughed as the door swung open a second time.

Ivan walked in, also wearing a towel and *shapka*. He took the bench across from us. “What is this, Dimitri? The kiddie *banya*? Where is the heat?”

Dimitri leaned back and spread his knees. “Not all is the same as in Russia. This is as close to a decent bathhouse as we will find, and do not think about running bare-assed into the snow outside to cool down. These Americans are stuck up. They use the showers.”

The stone oven hissed as water dripped down on the hot stones stacked deep inside. A spray of hot mist shot out from the top.

Wiping the sweat from my face, I asked, “So, what have we learned?”

Vaska gestured to Ivan. “Dimitri showed you the CQs and CQ-As yesterday?”

Ivan nodded.

Vaska continued. “What do you think?”

Ivan shrugged. “I think what you think. They are a bunch of cheap crap M16s and M4s from China, but I do not share your concern that they will cause us any problems. As I told Dimitri, let the bastards shoot their little dicks off with their cheap toys. They will come back to us for the real thing *and pay any price* when they are done fucking around.”

Vaska shook his head. “They are not a problem now, but mark my words, friend, they will become one.”

Wanting to avoid a disagreement, I offered, “Why not just take care of things now and avoid an issue in the future? Send a message.”

Vaska nodded. “I like that plan. We don’t have the name yet of the Chinese supplier in Chicago, but I’m certain those assholes the Petrov brothers know who it is.”

Ivan stood. "It is settled, then. When we learn the name, we will kill them and destroy the guns. Problem solved." He headed toward the door. "Time for a *platza*."

We each returned to the men's locker room and gestured to the attendant. He nodded and left the room. Moving deeper into the space, we each laid facedown on a towel-covered table. Three large women walked in, each carrying a bundle of eucalyptus leaves that were wet from being soaked in warm water.

As they each slapped us around the back and shoulders with the branches, our conversation continued. Turning my head to the side, I asked Dimitri, "Are you worried about blowback?"

He smirked. "Nothing we couldn't handle, I'm sure. Worst-case scenario, we'll call Gregor in for reinforcements. He's due for a visit to Chicago anyway."

Vaska added, "If you can pry him away from that adorable little girl of his. Did you see the photo he sent?"

Dimitri smiled. "I did. I told him if I have a girl, mine will be cuter."

Vaska laughed. "If you have a girl, the universe will tremble the moment she turns sixteen."

They both laughed.

Ivan and I exchanged looks. What happened to talking about whores, liquor, and guns?

"You two are like two old babushkas trading recipes," taunted Ivan.

Dimitri waved the women off and sat up, adjusting the towel around his hips. "You are one to talk. How was your dinner with Dylan?"

Ivan turned his face away. "Fine."

Vaska chuckled. "Fine? That was you I got a call about, from our contact in the Chicago police, wasn't it?"

Ivan shrugged. "A little misunderstanding. She thought

she was free to go out to dinner with some other man. She now knows differently."

Vaska nodded his head in Ivan's direction as he spoke to Dimitri. "Yes, a *little* misunderstanding. He damn near chopped some idiot's hand off at a downtown restaurant last night."

Dimitri shrugged into his robe as he took off his *shapka*. "Still claiming she's only a piece of ass you're banging for some fun while you're here?"

Ivan swung his legs off the table and stood up. He stalked toward Dimitri, fists clenched. "Don't talk about Dylan that way."

The atmosphere in the room was tense. Until Dimitri laughed and slapped Ivan on the back. "Welcome to the club, my friend."

The three of them chuckled as they strolled off toward the locker rooms.

I shook my head. Fools. Allowing themselves to be led around by the dick by some woman.

I checked the clock on the wall. I had better hurry. I was meeting the locksmith over at Carinna's apartment. As I slipped off the table and shrugged into my robe, I paused, then shook off the feeling that I was no better than Ivan, Vaska, and Dimitri right now. Nonsense. I was in complete control of my woman.

* * *

As I entered the hallway leading to Carinna's apartment, I could tell something was off. I reached behind me and pulled my handgun free from my back holster. I pulled the slide to load a round into the firing chamber and kept the gun in front of me. I walked slowly toward her door. As I passed Dylan's door, I cursed. It was clear someone had knocked it in earlier today. The new locks were busted, and the wood splintered. I kicked the door open and checked inside. There were signs of violence, but Dylan was not at home.

I raced across the hall and double-checked Carinna's door. It was locked and everything looked normal.

I took out my phone and called Ivan. "We have a problem."

Ivan spoke rapidly. "I already know. I've called Vaska. Meet us at the warehouse."

"You got it. I just have to make one stop."

I put my phone away and ran down the stairwell to my car.

I broke all the American traffic rules, racing to Carinna's school.

CHAPTER 12

arinna

Chef Paulina's voice continued in her usual slow and even pace. "The key to making perfect macarons is to have all your ingredients measured before you begin. Make sure your eggs are at room temperature before you carefully separate the whites."

I cracked the first egg and shattered a piece of shell. Cursing, I switched to a clean bowl and cracked a second egg. This one shattered as well, getting small fragments of shell in the whites. "Dammit."

My friend Avery shifted closer to me as she slid her bowl across the stainless steel counter we shared. "What's going on with you this morning?"

My cheeks heated. "Nothing."

"Nothing? I could cook an egg on your face right now."

I snorted. "Charming."

She gasped. "You were with a *boy*!" She said the last word in a singsong manner.

"I wasn't with a boy," I objected as I ruined yet another egg. I glanced up to make sure Chef Paulina hadn't seen.

What I said was totally true. The last thing anyone would call Maxim was a boy. An arrogant, possessive, domineering, sexy-as-hell but equally irritating-as-hell man, yes, but not a boy.

Avery took the egg from my hand and cracked it for me, skillfully separating the yolk from the white. As she picked up another egg, she said, "Come on. My dry spell was almost as long as yours… spill it."

I bit my lip. I was dying to talk to someone, and Dylan had answered none of my texts yet. Avery was as close to me as Dylan. In fact, we had often talked about going into business together once we had our pastry degrees. "Fine, yes, I was with someone last night."

She squealed.

Chef Paulina looked over at our station. "Ladies, have you sifted your almond flour and powdered sugar yet?"

"No, Chef. Working on it, Chef," we said in unison.

I measured out my almond flour. "You know my friend Dylan, right?"

She nodded as she too sifted her flour and sugar.

"Well, long story short, there were these two Russian guys she sort of… met… and one of them showed up at my bar last night."

"Was he Russian hot like Sean Bean in *GoldenEye* or Russian creepy like General Orlov from *Octopussy*?"

Avery had a super weird thing for James Bond films, especially Pierce Brosnan ones.

Setting my flour aside, I slowly poured my egg whites into the metal mixing bowl. "I have absolutely no idea who either of those people are. He was hot like Henry Cavill but with a crazy number of scary tattoos."

Chef Paulina cut in. "Remember to whip your egg whites until they are nice and foamy *before* you add the cream of tartar."

The small kitchen classroom echoed with the whir and buzz of mixers as each student started theirs at roughly the same time.

"So how was the sex?" asked Avery as she started up her mixer.

My cheeks heated even hotter. "It was… fine… good."

I mean, sure, it was the best sex of my freaking life, but it was also the most intense and kind of BDSM-y sex I'd ever had too.

Her head tilted back as she laughed. "You are turning beet red. Holy shit. Did you do butt stuff?"

Outraged, I objected. "No! I didn't do butt stuff!"

Not that Maxim hadn't threatened to fuck me in the ass later.

She shook her head and wagged her finger at me. "You totally did butt stuff."

Having already added my superfine sugar and whipped my egg whites into nice, firm peaks, I turned off my mixer. Unfortunately, so had everyone else when I blurted out loudly enough to be heard over the previous whir of the mixers, "I did not do butt stuff!"

Chef Paulina's mouth twitched. "That's good to know, Carinna. Now if you don't mind. I'd like to get back to your lesson."

I lowered my head and hunched my shoulders. "Yes, Chef."

Avery mouthed to me, "Sorry!"

I mouthed back, "You suck!"

Chef Paulina admonished the class. "Do not be too liberal

with your food coloring or extracts, ladies. Macarons should have a delicate color and flavoring."

I mixed my red and blue food coloring to make a pale lavender, which would complement the lavender and vanilla extract I was using for my recipe.

Avery was slowly folding yellow food coloring into her egg white mixture. "So, are you going to see him again?"

I shot her a horrified look. "Absolutely not."

"Why not?"

Once again, Chef Paulina cut in. "Your mixture should be slightly loose once you have mixed in your coloring, sugar, and flour. If it is still very firm, then it is under-mixed and you need to start over. If not, begin filling your piping bags."

I snatched my cloth piping bag and folded the edges over my left hand as I carefully spooned the mixture with my right. "Because he was a one-night stand. Trust me, this guy isn't dating material."

Avery adjusted the round tip to her piping bag and then followed suit. "So what? Why not just have some fun with him? Not every guy has to be boyfriend material."

I almost blurted out that I had thought the exact same thing... until… well, until everything.

Seeing him naked.

His enormous cock with its intimidating reverse Prince Albert piercing.

His domineering, controlling way in bed.

The way he pulled my hair and spanked my ass.

Oh, yeah, and the way he threatened to kill any man that looked at me.

Of course, he had bought me groceries and made me coffee this morning. Those things were very boyfriend-like. And the way he made sure I was buckled in was very sweet. If he wasn't such a big, scary dude, I might even think him driving me to school and picking me up was romantic.

Still, it was hard to avoid all the flapping red flags.

Nope. I was better off walking away now.

Ignoring her comment, I asked, "Can I stay at your place tonight?"

Avery nodded. "Sure. I want to practice my coconut chocolate marjolaine with you. I can't seem to get the layers perfectly even."

"We'll swing by the store and grab the ingredients and a frozen pizza."

"It's a date," smiled Avery. "Of course, you could be having a date with hot Russian dude, instead of me."

I stuck my tongue out at her and concentrated on piping my macarons evenly onto my parchment paper-lined sheet pan.

The classroom was quiet as we all concentrated on our task.

Suddenly, there was a loud clatter outside in the hall. As if someone had slammed a heavy door open. There were voices raised in anger and the sounds of a scuffle.

Chef Paulina frowned. Scanning over the classroom, she instructed, "Continue with your task, class. I will see what is the matter."

As she neared the classroom door, it swung open violently. The door hit the cement wall so hard the frosted panel of glass cracked.

A sick feeling of dread settled in my stomach. No. It couldn't be. Please, God, don't let it be him.

Chef Paulina stepped back a few paces as she called out, "What is the meaning of this?"

Maxim stepped over the threshold.

My upper body dipped forward as I gripped the edge of my stainless steel counter, afraid I would faint. Again. That was twice in two days. Never in my life had I ever had cause to faint before meeting Maxim.

He flashed his perfect set of white teeth at her. I'm sure Chef Paulina viewed it as a normal smile. I saw it for what it really was… a wolf's grin.

"I need Carinna to come with me."

Chef Paulina pressed her hand to her chest as she giggled. Yes, giggled.

Before she could respond, our beer-bellied security guard, Sam, burst into the room. "Sorry, Chef Paulina, he wouldn't take no for an answer."

Chef Paulina surveyed Maxim up and down. "No, I don't suppose he would."

Wait. What was happening?

Was my sixty-something and very married teacher *flirting* with Maxim?

Now instead of fainting, I thought I would vomit.

And why did I feel a stab of jealousy at the idea of it?

Chef Paulina continued, "I'm afraid we're in the middle of class."

Maxim tilted his head down and stared at her. "Make an exception."

Chef Paulina giggled again.

Oh, for the love of…

Maxim turned and surveyed the classroom.

I ducked under the table.

Avery nudged me with her foot. "Is that him?" she whispered urgently.

"Shhhh."

She nudged me again. This time, her voice raised an entire octave. "Carinna, he's coming this way. What do I do?"

CHAPTER 13

axim

I STORMED DOWN THE AISLE, which was flanked by neat rows of stainless steel tables, each with a staring student dressed in a white chef's coat. They looked like identical little dolls. It was, however, easy to find *my* doll. She was the one unsuccessfully hiding from me under the table.

As I neared, she attempted to crawl away, leaving a trail of disturbed flour and sugar in her wake.

Another female stepped in front of me, blocking my path.

"Carinna… um… she… well… she, um… she left already."

I smiled down at the petite thing with freckles and a mass of bright red hair that was barely contained under her black chef's hat. She was cute, but not my style. No, my style was a curvy woman with flashing blue eyes and long curly honey-brown hair with a mouth that would bring a man to his knees.

I leaned down and tapped the edge of Freckles' nose. "What is your name?"

She twisted her chef's coat between her hands as she anxiously cast a glance over her shoulder where Carinna was still trying to not-so-stealthily evade me. "Avery."

"Avery," I repeated. It suited her. "I will remember this."

Say what you want about these American women. They certainly were fearless when it came to protecting their friends. It was highly admirable. One of the first things that caught my eye about Carinna was how she had been willing to stand up to me to protect Dylan. No small feat. I had seen larger, far more brutal men cower in my presence, but not her. And now, this little sprite was foolishly jumping in to protect Carinna. It pleased me she had such a loyal and brave friend.

Although, right now, I had no patience for such things.

Dylan was in danger, which meant Carinna might be as well.

Until Ivan and I knew precisely what was going on, both women were going into lockdown whether or not they liked it.

I gently cupped Avery's shoulders and lifted her high and to the right, out of my path. I easily caught up with Carinna. Without even stopping, I swooped down and twisted a large section of her chef's coat in my hand and lifted her right off the floor like a duffle bag.

Carinna wiggled in my grasp and protested. "Hey! Let go! Stop!"

Ignoring her pleas, I raised a farewell hand to her teacher. "It is a game we play."

Her teacher giggled and waved back. "What fun!"

I carried Carinna out of the classroom and down the hallway. When it was clear she would not stop screaming, I threw open a nearby door. It was a small office with an elderly man behind the desk. "Get out."

Without asking a single question, he jumped up to obey.

I placed Carinna on her feet in the middle of the office and turned back to close and lock the door.

Her chef's cap was long gone. She used her forearm to toss her errant curls away from her face as she forcefully pulled down on her chef's coat to straighten it. "What is the meaning of this?" she huffed, still out of breath from her struggle.

I wasn't in the habit of explaining myself to the women of my acquaintance, but I would make this one exception for her. "There is a problem. I need to get you someplace safe."

"Whatever problem there may be, it is clearly your problem, not mine. I'm going back to class."

She tried to storm past me. I held up an arm, blocking her path. "You're not going anywhere."

Carinna crossed her arms over her chest and paced away from me. I didn't want to tell her just yet, but clearly, I had no choice. "The problem is with Dylan."

She turned around with a snap. "What about Dylan? Did your friend Ivan hurt her? I'll kill him if he did."

Ruthlessly hiding a smile at the thought of my little Carinna attacking Ivan with her tiny fists, I shook my head no. "There was an issue at her apartment this morning. It sounds as if her uncle may be involved."

Carinna visibly relaxed. "Is that all?"

My brow furrowed. I took a step closer. "I don't think you understand. Someone trashed her apartment."

Carinna shrugged. "Her family are assholes. It's not the first time her uncle or her piece of shit cousin came by and started trouble. They've even trashed the place before. That's why she doesn't have nice things. We'll handle it."

I hadn't wanted to alarm her, but apparently it was necessary to get her cooperation. "He gave her a black eye."

Carinna let out an exasperated sigh. "Is that what this is all about? Dylan knows how to cover up a black eye, just like I do." She waved her hand up and down in front of her in my direction. "I don't know where this misplaced chivalry is coming from, but Dylan and I take care of each other. We always have. We'll handle this. We don't need *you* interfering. Now, get out of my way. I'm going back to class."

I heard nothing past *just like I do*.

I could literally feel the blood pumping through my veins as a pain like a steel spike went straight through my temples. My hands curled into fists as my vision blurred. Someone had hit her. And not just once. You don't get cavalier about a black eye unless it's happened to you more than once.

Someone had hit her.

Someone had hit her.

Hit her.

Someone had *fucking* hit her.

It pounded around my skull like a sick drumbeat until I wanted to let out a primal scream of rage.

Someone had hit her. My Carinna. *Moya malen'kaya iskra.*

I took several steps toward her.

She glanced down at my closed fists, fear evident in her gaze despite her bravado.

My stomach twisted as I forced myself to unclench my fingers. I cornered her against the wall.

I raised my arms.

She started as she twisted her head away. "What are you doing?"

"Tsss, moya malyshka, prosto pozvol'mne sdelat' eto." I hadn't even realized I slipped into my mother tongue as I carefully placed my hands on her cheeks. Cupping her jaw, I tilted her

head back to stare into her beautiful ocean blue eyes. *"Nikto nikogda prinesot tebe bol' opyat'. Ya dayu tebe slovo."*

I stroked her cheekbones with my thumbs as I pushed my fingers deeper into her soft curls.

She licked her lips, drawing my gaze to her mouth.

Her breathing became shallow. "I don't know what you are saying."

I leaned down and gently pressed my lips to hers. "You have my word. No one will ever hurt you again, my sweet babygirl. I will make sure of it. Any man who raises his fist to you will die by my hand. Do you understand me?"

She tilted her head. Her breath mingled with mine as her lips opened for me. "That is an empty promise. We barely know one another. Why would you say something like that?"

I wrapped an arm around her waist and lifted her high against my body. Instinctively, she wrapped her legs around my hips. Turning, I swiped my arm across the desk, sending a laptop and several files crashing to the floor. I laid her back on the smooth wooden surface.

I ran my hand down the back of her leg and pulled off her right sneaker before doing the same to the left. I then flipped up her chef's coat and reached for the waistband of her yoga pants.

"Wait! We can't! Not here!"

I leaned down and kissed her bare belly. "This is happening, babygirl. Apparently, I need to show you just how well I do know you."

I pulled down her panties with her yoga pants.

Soft winter sunlight streamed in through the heavy slats of the dark wood blinds over our heads, illuminating her pale, creamy skin. The whir of the mixers nearby and the sounds of chatter just outside the door gave the small office an otherworldly cocoon-like feel, as if we were the only two people in the world.

I knew the men were waiting. I knew, despite Carinna's assurances that it was no big deal, that we would deal with Dylan's uncle in a very real and very violent manner. But all that could wait. Right at this moment it was just me and Carinna and I had something very important to prove to my little spitfire.

I draped one of her legs over my shoulder and placed a restraining hand on her stomach. Leaning between her sleek thighs, using the ball of my piercing gently to part her open, I licked the smooth seam of her pussy. Glancing up over her body, I gave her a wink. "So sweet."

I flicked my tongue over her clit in a slow, steady rhythm, building her response, knowing the smooth metal ball was hitting in all the right ways. Her moans were like oxygen to me. I increased the pressure. Her thigh clenched against the side of my head. I knew she was close.

Rising, I shrugged out of my suit jacket. As I unbuckled my belt, I looked down at her and commanded, "Touch yourself."

Her pretty cheeks pinkened. Her hand tentatively moved over her abdomen to barely tease the top of her pussy.

"No, my darling." Dropping my belt buckle, I leaned over and snatched her wrist. Bringing her hand to my mouth, I sucked two fingers in deep. Swirling my tongue around each one, wetting them. I then pulled her fingers free and placed them over her pussy. "I want you to *touch* yourself."

I returned to my belt buckle and pulled the belt free through my pant loops. I ran my hand over the thin strap of shiny black leather. Meant for dress pants, it was too thin and hard to whip her with, although my cock lengthened at the thought of it. Later tonight, I would break out my worn brown leather belt. I couldn't wait to see her cry and writhe as I strapped her luscious ass till it gleamed a bright cherry red. Oh, yes, she would be punished for trying to defy me earlier, just not now. Now I had other plans for my babygirl.

Tossing the belt aside, I reached for my zipper. Watching her reaction, I slowly lowered it and pulled out my cock. I fisted the length as I watched her golden-brown eyes widen. I knew she still wasn't used to the length and girth of my shaft, let alone the evil-looking metal hardware dangling from the tip.

Pushing her fingers away, I used the metal hoop and ball to taunt her clit. "That's it baby, come for me. Come on my cock."

Her hips rose off the desk as she pushed herself against the piercing and the tip of my cock.

Her fingers gripped the edges of the desk. "Oh, fuck, fuck, fuck!" She rocked back and forth.

Placing two fingers in my mouth, I wet them before pushing against her entrance. Sliding them inside, I curled them ever so slightly, teasing her soft, sensitive inner walls. "Say my name, baby. I want to hear you cry out to me."

Her head lolled from side to side. "Fuck… Maxim!"

The very moment I heard her sweet lips cry my name, I plunged my cock deep into her tight pussy, burying myself straight to the hilt, forcing her to take each and every thick inch. The desk's legs squeaked as it shifted across the floor with each thrust of my hips.

I was fucking her too hard. She was going to tear if I wasn't careful, and yet I couldn't make myself stop. She was so wet and tight. I placed my flat palms on either side of her hips and pounded into her pliable body. I needed her to understand, needed her to know that she was mine now, and that I always protected what was mine. Never again would I allow anyone close enough to hurt her.

I felt like this should have scared the shit out of me, but it didn't.

Something just felt right about wanting to keep her close and protect her.

My cock swelled as pressure built in my balls. I tore open her chef's coat and lifted her T-shirt and scarf. Pushing up her bra, I latched onto one perfect pink nipple. I pulled it in deep and scraped the sensitive flesh with my teeth. She came a second time just as I unleashed deep inside her sweet cunt.

For the first time in my life, I came inside a woman without a condom on, and didn't give a damn about the consequences.

* * *

AFTER WE FINISHED, I helped her dress. Pulling her close to my side, I escorted her out of the building to my car. Once she was inside, I reached past her into the glove compartment. I pulled out a roll of duct tape.

Carinna's eyes widened. "What are you doing?"

I tore off a strip. "Sorry, baby. It has to be done."

CHAPTER 14

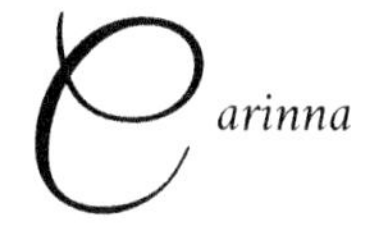

arinna

"HMMFR$%&# MFFFTHHPFTT $&#$MPFFT!"

Maxim leaned in and kissed my duct-taped lips. "I know, baby. I won't be long. As soon as I'm done, I'll take you out for a nice dinner. Do you like oysters? I hear a place called Shaw's has some nice ones."

I pulled on my duct-taped wrists, which were lashed to my ankles as I screamed. "MFGH#$&PT MDS$TH!"

He brushed my hair, which was now just a wild mass of spiral curls, from my eyes. "Struggling will only make things worse."

I growled low in my throat as I narrowed my gaze on him.

He chuckled as he got out of the car.

I watched in fury as he strolled up to several more Russian men. They laughed and pointed in my direction as they greeted him. Apparently, it was no big deal to see

Maxim roll up with a female captive duct taped in his passenger seat. They even passed around a flask. Seriously, what the fuck?

I rocked back and forth as I pulled on my wrists. The car shimmied with my movements, but the tape didn't budge. I was well and truly caught.

It had all happened so fast.

One moment I was crawling through a flour- and sugar-covered floor, trying to get away from him. The next I was having an amazing screaming orgasm on the dean of students' desk. And then I was somehow duct taped and riding toward a super shady warehouse in an even shadier part of Chicago I hadn't even known existed.

When we had gotten into the car, like an idiot, I thought Maxim was leaning in for another kiss. When I saw the duct tape, it took a moment for my brain to register what was happening, because after all, no matter how many true crime documentaries a girl may watch on her Saturday off, she doesn't automatically think *I'm being kidnapped* when she sees a roll of duct tape. Before I knew it, he had my wrists bound. As I struggled to get free, he easily wrapped a strip around my feet and connected it to my wrists. I wasn't exactly hogtied, but I wasn't exactly not hogtied either.

He taped my mouth shut next, careful to avoid catching my hair. What a gentleman.

I didn't care if he could understand me or not. I ranted and railed at him the entire time, but he wouldn't budge. Fortunately, I stopped long enough for him to read a text message from Ivan letting me know Dylan was safe and with someone named Mary.

Now I was staring at him having a cozy chat with two other extremely big, tatted-up men. Was one of these men Ivan? Probably. I couldn't believe I tried to convince Dylan to go out with him. I couldn't believe I convinced myself that a quick one-night stand with Maxim would be *fun* and no big deal!

Never in my life had I been so wrong about so many things in such a short period of time.

Somehow, I had to think of a way to get Dylan and myself out of this mess. I had to come up with a plan. Something not as extreme as *Thelma and Louise,* but also not involving us going into the witness protection program and living the rest of our lives as Mary Sue and Betty Lou deep in the middle of Kansas working at some no-name diner. Although that may be unavoidable. There wasn't a doubt in my mind that I was staring at some high-level criminals, and Maxim was right there in the mix.

I had little experience with these things. Dylan was the one with the criminal family. My family was just a bunch of heartless, bloodsucking assholes, but I was fairly certain I knew a pack of Russian mafia men when I saw them.

Once again, I tried to lift my wrists above my waist. It was no good. They wouldn't reach. I tried leaning down, but they were too low. Dammit, I needed to get to the gym more often. If I had kept up with that stupid yoga class, maybe I'd be able to bend myself into a pretzel and get these stupid binds off.

A cry drew my attention to the left.

Two men in suits entered the loading dock area of the warehouse, dragging a man between them. The man was beaten bloody and his clothes were shredded and torn as if he had been thrown through a glass window. With a start, I recognized him. He was Dylan's uncle. Not the one who sent her the money. He was supposedly still in Russia, but the other one. I couldn't remember his name.

His feet dragged behind him as he sagged between the men. As they neared Maxim and the other men, it was clear he was pleading for his life.

Maxim captured my gaze from across the loading dock.

Instead of appearing like their usual bright emerald, his eyes looked cold and black.

Oh, my God, they were going to kill him.

They were going to kill Dylan's uncle right in front of me.

My eyes widened. I screamed, even though it was muffled by the duct tape. I slammed my body against the passenger door. Maxim gestured in my direction and then motioned his head to the right. They dragged Dylan's uncle out of view. Maxim cast one more look in my direction before following them, but not before gesturing to another man in a suit nearby and then to the car.

The man strolled up. I wasn't dumb enough to think he was going to set me free, although my heart gave a little jump at the thought. No such luck. He stood several feet away and guarded the car. So much for the chance of me loosening this tape and escaping while they were out of sight.

It felt like an eternity before Maxim returned.

His suit jacket and tie were both off. His shirtsleeves were rolled up, exposing more of his ominous tattoos. You could see the faint outline of his silver nipple piercings and chest tattoos through the thin pale violet of his shirt. As he walked closer to the car, I saw something else.

Blood splatter.

Oh, my God.

He passed on the driver's side and went straight to the trunk, opening it. Several minutes ticked by. When he closed the trunk, he was wearing a black pullover sweater with his same gray dress slacks.

He opened the car door and slid inside.

I stilled.

Without saying a word, he reached into the car console and pulled out a stiletto knife. He flicked the blade open. There was absolutely no rational reason why I shouldn't have been deathly afraid at that moment. I mean, I was fairly certain he had just helped kill my friend's uncle in cold blood, and yet I wasn't. Somehow, I knew he wasn't going to hurt me. Not really. But that didn't mean I wasn't going to try to escape the very moment I had a chance.

Maxim could be sexy and sweet, but he was also obviously a very dangerous and intense man. Too intense for me. His life wasn't like mine. I wanted a normal nine-to-five type of guy. The kind who didn't carry around duct tape in his murder bag.

Maxim leaned over and carefully sliced the blade through the tape around my ankles. Then my wrists. He balled the tape up and tossed it into the back seat. Then, using both hands, he gingerly pulled it off my mouth.

He cupped my cheek and ran his thumb over my sore lips. "Never make me do that again, babygirl."

I was trying to be brave for both Dylan and myself, but this was all just too much.

He was too close. My body's reaction to him was too confusing.

All I wanted to do in that moment was curl up in a ball and cry.

What was so terrifying was that I wanted to do that in his arms.

I needed to get away from him as soon as possible. This man was toxic as hell.

My eyes teared up. "Please, just let me go."

He ran his thumb over my lips a second time. "No."

CHAPTER 15

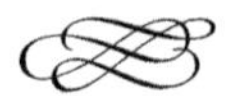

*arinna*

THROUGH THE REFLECTION in the passenger side mirror, I watched the high-rises of Chicago fade into the distance. Maxim raced north on the highway. Less than a half hour later, we got off at the Evanston exit. We entered a gated community. After passing several massive McMansions, he pulled up to what I could only describe as the most antisocial-looking one of the bunch. A tall brick wall surrounded the entire property, ending at a huge wrought-iron gate blocking the driveway. Pitched every few feet along the top of the wall was a security camera.

The gates slowly opened, and Maxim drove forward.

I watched in horror as the gates closed the moment the car passed. Once they snapped shut, I would be well and truly trapped. Before Maxim had even stopped the car in front of the house, in one fluid motion, I snapped my seat belt off and opened the car door.

I stumbled, landing painfully on my right knee as my sneakers slipped on the gravel, but quickly righted myself and ran for the gate like the hounds of hell were chasing me.

I didn't dare spare a glance over my shoulder.

I knew Maxim was fast on my heels by his angry shout.

I tucked my head down and ran faster. My lungs were on fire as the muscles in my legs screamed, but I pressed on.

There was only about a two-foot gap in the gate now.

I was still about fifty yards away.

Fuck, I wasn't going to make it.

The ominous sound of crunching gravel taunted me as Maxim's larger stride brought him within a hair's breadth of me.

My lungs seized.

The gap was only a foot wide now.

I was so close.

I stretched out my right arm, hoping the motion sensors would stop the gate. If I could make it through before it closed, then Maxim would have to wait for it to reopen. Those few extra seconds would be just enough time for me to scream to get a neighbor's or passing car's attention.

My shoulder and right foot passed through the gate.

I was almost free.

A sharp pain wrenched my head back.

Maxim had fisted my hair and pulled me toward him.

The unchecked reverse motion had my body flying backward.

Still keeping his grip on my hair, he hooked his arm to force my body into the safety of his own as his torso twisted. His shoulder took the brunt of our first impact on the gravel driveway. He rolled, keeping me tucked close as we landed several feet away in the grass under a tree with him on top of me.

Maxim straddled my hips and grabbed my head. "Are you hurt?"

I coughed as oxygen rushed back into my lungs.

"Dammit, Carinna, are you hurt?"

He ran his hands over my body, checking for broken bones or other serious injuries.

"I'm fine," I coughed again. "I'm fine!"

He pounded the ground over my head with his fist. "What the fuck were you thinking?"

Just as angry, I fired back, "I was thinking I'd get away from the homicidal criminal who kidnapped me and just killed my friend's uncle!"

He gripped my throat just below my jaw and leaned in close. "I got news for you, babygirl. I'm not just a homicidal criminal. I'm also the man who just had his cock deep inside this pussy of yours." He reached down with his other hand and palmed me between my legs. "That means I own you."

I bucked but couldn't dislodge him. "The fuck it does!"

Maxim laughed. It was a hollow sound with no mirth. He leaned up and reached for his belt buckle. "Want me to prove it to you again?"

My chest rose and fell with each heated, angry breath I took. "You're just a guy I fucked. You don't *own me* any more than the next guy I fuck does."

My taunt was true, or at least it should have been true.

Why did it feel like a lie?

He whipped off his belt and wrapped it around my throat. Not tight enough to cut off my air, more like he was putting a collar on me. I reached up to grip the leather and pull it away from my neck. He snatched my wrists and wrenched my arms over my head using just one hand. With the other, he maintained a tight grip on the end of the leather strap.

When he finally spoke, his words were as sharp as cut

glass. "You let another man touch you and that is the last thing he will do on this earth."

My eyes filled with tears. "Why are you doing this?"

The hard angles of his face softened slightly. "Believe it or not, baby, I'm trying to protect you."

"I never needed protection until you came along."

"That's a goddamn lie and you know it. It's true we just met, and I know nothing about your past any more than you know about mine, but any woman who thinks a black eye is no big deal is someone who needed protection and didn't get it."

Images of my father and mother taking out their rage-filled hate on me with their fists after my brother's death floated unwanted across my mind's eye. My stomach twisted. My older brother had been my protector, but on that fateful night five years ago, I killed him. And I would forever pay the price for that. I didn't deserve a protector, not even a dangerous criminal one.

Feeling my body slacken, Maxim loosened his grip. "We don't get to choose the people we feel a connection to. You're smart and beautiful and ambitious and you deserve a man who works an ordinary nine-to-five job who will give you kids and a dog and a white picket fence—but you didn't get that. You got me instead."

I sniffed as a stray tear ran down my cheek. "You could still choose to let me go."

Maxim smiled. "No, *moya lyubimaya,* I couldn't. From the moment I first set eyes on you... I don't think I had a choice."

He spoke the words calmly, almost philosophically, as if he wasn't speaking to me, but rather uttering a realization to himself.

"What does that mean? Loo bi maya?"

Maxim unwrapped the belt from my neck and stood. He fed it through his belt loops and buckled it before reaching down to haul me to my feet. Pressing me close to his body, he placed a hand on my jaw and tilted my head back. "Beloved."

He took my hand in his and led me back to the house. In a daze, I willingly followed. As we neared the entrance, the door opened. A slim, elderly woman with her salt and pepper hair tied back in a tight bun, wearing a black dress covered with a crisp white apron, opened the door. "Mr. Miloslavsky, welcome. Mr. Ivanov told me to expect you."

Maxim shot me a stern look before mouthing, "Behave."

I narrowed my eyes and resisted the urge to stick my tongue out at him, which, knowing him, he'd take as an invitation.

Maxim pulled me over the threshold into the dark interior before saying, "Hello, Rose. Thank you. Is the room prepared?"

Rose locked the door behind us. She gestured for us to follow her down the hallway. She opened a door on the right. There was a steep staircase that led down into the basement. "Yes, sir," she cheerily replied. "You'll be pleased to know Mr. Ivanov installed all new soundproofing last spring, so no one will hear a thing."

A soundproof room located down a creepy staircase into a basement?

I opened my mouth to object, but it was too late.

Maxim pulled me down the first few steps.

Terrified, I looked behind me to see Rose close the door, casting us both into darkness.

CHAPTER 16

Maxim

The moment we reached the bottom stair, overhead fluorescent lights clicked on, one by one, track by track until the entire underground bunker was illuminated. If I knew one thing about my friend Gregor, he did nothing by half measure. The last time I was here, this was a stripped-down cement basement with a bare concrete floor. The cinder block walls were riddled with chips and holes from all the bullets. Apparently, since then he had completely remodeled the place into a state-of-the-art private luxury gun range.

They'd lined the walls with sound-abatement wood paneling. Row upon row of semi-automatic rifles and handguns from just about every country that officially made them, and a few that unofficially did, hung from small black hooks: Borchardt C-93s, Fusil Automatique Modele 1917s, Gewehr 43s, CZ-75s, Mondragon rifles, Smith & Wesson M&P 15s, and of course the usual AR-15s including a

Heckler and Koch MR556 and Sig Sauer M400. He even had a personal favorite of mine, the Barrett REC7. A crate of the Dragunov rifles Ivan and I had just sold to Vaska and Dimitri was stacked against the wall in the corner. I'm sure it was payment for some service rendered.

But it was the handguns I was most interested in. Keeping a firm grip on Carinna's hand, I led her past two workbenches that had various tools and gun parts scattered about them to the back wall where Gregor displayed several varieties of handguns: Glock 22s, Kimber Stainless Raptor IIs, Ruger Blackhawks, Ruger SP101s, and the Sig Sauer P220 Combat as well as a few classic Smith & Wesson revolvers, which were always good to have on hand when you wanted to intimidate someone with a round of Russian roulette.

I grabbed a Glock 42 and a Smith & Wesson Model 642 with the stainless steel barrel and synthetic black grip. My personal Glock was a 41. It had a nine-inch slide with about five and half inches of that being the barrel. It was far too large for her small hands. Not to mention it being a .45 caliber and weighing about two pounds fully loaded. Carinna needed something small she could manage. I then turned toward the bins under the nearest workbench to look for ammunition.

"Are you going to kill me?"

With a sigh, I reached for my Glock, which was secured in a waistband holster at the small of my back. I checked the magazine and pulled back the slide, chambering a bullet. I then turned the gun around and held it in front of Carinna. "Take it."

She tried to back up a step as she raised her palms. "I don't want—"

I grabbed her upper arm and dragged her closer. Snatching her wrist, I held her arm chest high and pressed the gun into her palm. "I said take it."

Her arm dipped from the unexpected weight. She grabbed at it with both hands, but kept it lowered.

I picked up her hands and leveled the gun at the center of my chest. "Do it. Pull the trigger."

All the color left her cheeks. She tried to back away, but my grip on her hands and the gun prevented it.

"What? No! You're mad."

I looked her square in the eyes. "Do it, Carinna. Pull the trigger."

She shook her head as she once again tried to drop the gun.

I pressed the barrel harder against my chest. "Do it. If you think I'm a danger to you. If you think I could truly harm you. Then pull the trigger."

Her eyes filled with tears, which spilled over onto her pale cheeks. "No. I'm not going to kill you."

I forced her finger over the trigger. "You think I'm going to kill you? Then pull the trigger. Save yourself. *Save yourself from me.*"

Tears glistened on her trembling lips. "I… I… no."

"Why not? I forced my way into your apartment. I kidnapped you. It's justified homicide. Self-defense. You want to get away from me so badly, just—"

She blinked as her arms shook. "No. I don't want to get away from you. I do, but I don't. Fuck, please don't make me do this. I just… you… you killed him! You killed him and broke that other guy's nose and… and… I don't know what to do or think. I don't…"

"I will not apologize for helping kill a piece of shit abuser who beat up your friend just as I will not apologize for breaking that asshole's nose for touching you. They both deserved what they got. And I'm sure as fuck not going to apologize for wanting to protect you. I protect what's mine."

She raised the gun higher and straightened her arms,

locking her elbows. She then swiped her shoulder over her left cheek to wipe away the tears. Her lips thinned as she backed away one step. "I'm not yours! Stop saying that!"

I moved forward, once more pressing the gun into the center of my chest. "No."

She backed away a second time. "Don't come any closer. I will shoot you. I will. I'll do it. You have to stop this. All of this. It's insane. Just let me go."

I slowly shook my head as I stepped forward again. "No."

She shook the gun at me. "Stop saying no. That's all you ever say."

My lips twisted into a smirk, my gaze traveling over her body as I responded suggestively, "Oh, *moya malen'kaya iskra,* that's not all I ever say."

All the color rushed back into her cheeks. I knew she was remembering all the filthy things I said to her last night while I was balls deep in her sweet cunt, spanking her ass.

She had ditched the chef's coat and scarf and was standing in front of me in a thin, long-sleeved T-shirt that hugged her tits nicely and a pair of black yoga pants that showed off the curve of her hips and her long, sleek legs. My cock hardened just remembering those legs wrapped around my waist as I carried her over to the desk earlier, before fucking her senseless.

Damn, this woman was in my blood. I couldn't get enough of her sassy mouth or that tight pussy. Never in my life had a woman dared to challenge me like she had. Of course, none had tried their hardest to run from me either. Usually it was the other way around. It was intoxicating just being near her. Not knowing what she would do or say from one moment to the next. She was like trying to hold a flame. *Moya malen'kaya iskra. My little spark. My spitfire.* And yes, she was mine. Every cheeky, feisty inch of her.

Even at this moment, there was a fifty-fifty chance she could actually pull the trigger.

"It's now or never, baby. Pull the trigger and you end it all."

She sniffed as she wiped her other cheek with her shoulder. Her beautiful lips trembled.

I took another step closer. Her elbows bent as her grip slackened. I held her gaze with mine. "But know this, babygirl. If you don't. That's it. Game over. You're mine." I reached down and cupped my hard cock through my slacks. "And I'm going to make damn sure you never forget who owns you."

She gasped as her wrists dipped. The gun swung slack between her fingers.

I snatched it from her hand and tossed it onto a nearby workbench as I reached out my arm and cupped my hand around the back of her neck. Fisting her hair at the nape, I pulled her forward till her body slammed into mine. Before she could say a word, my mouth crashed down onto hers. I tasted the salt of her tears as my tongue swept between her lips.

Breaking the kiss, I pulled on her hair, tilting her head back. "You've been a naughty girl this morning." I palmed her breast and squeezed. "I was going to wait till later, but I think my dirty girl needs a taste of my hand on her ass."

"Oh, God," she moaned against my mouth.

I ran my tongue over her lips. "Is that what you need, baby? Do you need me to show you what a dirty girl you are? You need to feel the sting of my palm on that cute ass of yours?"

Her eyelids fluttered closed as she breathed, "Maxim."

That was all I needed to hear.

Pushing my gun aside, I used my grip on her hair to bend her over the workbench. It was a low bench, so she bent at the waist, putting her at just the right height for my cock. I pulled her pants down to her ankles, exposing her ass. With the tips of my fingers, I lifted the thin strip of fabric between her cheeks and snapped it back into place. Her body jerked in response. I then lifted it again and tore the thong off her body. "I don't think I'm going to let you wear panties anymore," I whispered in her ear.

I ran my hand over the curve of her ass as I pushed my hips against her thigh, taunting her with the hard ridge of my cock. "Are you my dirty girl? Is this pussy wet for me?" I placed my hand between her thighs and teased the seam of her cunt with my fingertips.

She moaned in response and arched her back.

"Say it. Say you're a dirty girl who wants my cock."

Her forehead rolled from side to side against the smooth, cool surface of the workbench. "Please, don't make me say it. It's too humiliating."

I lifted my hand and spanked her right ass cheek.

Carinna yelped in surprise.

I spanked her left cheek, then her right again. With each strike, her ass jiggled suggestively. I spanked her harder, making sure to get the soft under-curve of her ass and the tops of her thighs.

"Ow! That hurts!"

"You're lucky it's not my belt." I continued to spank her ass, enjoying the view as her creamy flesh turned a bright cherry red. I caressed each cheek, relishing the warmth of her skin against my palm. "But it will be later tonight."

I watched as her sharp teeth bit down on her full bottom lip, stifling a response.

"Tonight, I'm going to tie you to the bed and lash this cute ass with my leather belt until you scream for mercy."

"Oh, God!"

"God cannot grant you mercy. Only me," I responded as I

undid my belt and tossed it aside. I lowered the zipper to my pants and pulled out my cock. I should have been sated from earlier, but I was a man possessed. Like a drug, I needed to feel the tight clasp of her pussy around my cock. Needed to prove to her in word and deed that she was now under my control. There would be no escape from me now.

Like the arrogant asshole I was, this time I wanted her to orgasm from my cock and not my tongue. Lifting my arm, I struck her ass with my open palm several more times, knowing the hot stinging pain would only heighten her awareness the moment I plunged my shaft deep into her body.

I tightened my grip on her hair as I positioned myself behind her. I wanted to feel her heated skin against my own, but that would have to wait till later. I fisted my cock and ran the head between her pussy lips, wetting the tip. "Feel that, baby? Beg for my cock. Beg like the little whore I know you are."

She nudged her hips back, opening for me as she groaned.

I slapped her ass. "I can't hear you."

"Please! Please fuck me!"

I teased her clit with the ball from my cock piercing. "Why? Tell me why, baby. Talk dirty to me."

She ground her ass against my hips. "Because I'm a dirty little whore who wants your cock."

I thrust in deep.

She cried out as her body rocked forward. Despite fucking her earlier, her pussy was just as impossibly tight. I could feel her inner walls clench around my shaft. I pulled back until I felt the band of muscle at her entrance clutch at the ridge of my shaft, before plunging in deep a second time.

I pulled her hair till her head fell between her shoulder blades and her back arched. "That's it. Take it. Take every inch like a good girl."

I thrust harder and faster as I spanked her ass several times.

"Maxim!"

I spread my hand over her lower back, then moved it over her ass. Opening her cheeks, I placed my thumb at her tight, puckered entrance, feeling the soft ridges as her body clenched the hole tight. "I'm taking your ass next. Have you ever done that, baby? Have you ever given this tight ass to any other man?"

She moaned, "Never."

I pushed my thumb inside, watching as the delicate dark pink skin around her asshole turned white.

"Ow! Ow! Take it out!"

"No."

I twisted my thumb inside her tight entrance, opening her as I continued to pound into her hot, wet cunt. The idea of taking her anal virginity later nearly had me spilling my seed. I clenched my teeth and prolonged the pleasurable torture a little longer. I would not come until she did.

I increased my pace. Our labored breathing echoed around the wood-paneled walls in the silent room.

"Oh… fuck! Fuck! I'm coming! Maxim."

I pushed my thumb in as deep as it would go. "That's my dirty girl. Come with my thumb in your ass and my cock in this hungry pussy of yours."

The moment she came, I lifted my arm and spanked her ass hard. I wanted her to associate pain with pleasure, needed her to know that was how it was always going to be with me. I liked it rough. I liked to hear her cries of pain as her body clenched down as wave after rippling wave hit her. I would always treat her like a whore in the bedroom, using her body for my own needs while satisfying hers. And I would never let her deny that was just like she wanted it. She was a dirty girl who liked her ass spanked and her hair pulled, and I wouldn't let her forget it.

My abdomen clenched as the pressure in my balls increased. This time, I pulled out. Using my grip on her hair, I pushed her to her knees. I placed my hand on her cheeks and squeezed, forcing her mouth open. Releasing her hair, I gripped my cock and aimed my seed at her open mouth. "Swallow every drop like my good little whore."

She choked as a thick stream hit the back of her throat. Finally, she swallowed.

I tightened my grip on her face. "Now lick your lips."

She boldly kept her eyes on me as she obeyed, seductively slipping the tip of her tongue over her bottom lip before gliding it over her upper lip. When she was finished, she winked.

At that moment, I wasn't entirely sure if I was still the one in control.

As dangerous as I was, I had a feeling she was far more dangerous.

CHAPTER 17

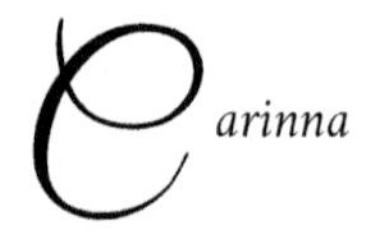
arinna

"Spread your legs a little wider," he instructed, as he placed his hands on my hips.

"Isn't that what you said earlier?" I teased.

He gave my still-sore ass a swat. "Pay attention. This is serious stuff now."

Less than an hour ago I was holding a gun to his chest while he taunted me to pull the trigger, but *now* we were going to be serious?

The shift in mood and intentions made me dizzy. I had a feeling it would always be that way with a man like Maxim. One moment I wanted to kill him, the next I wanted to run from him and the next I was begging him to fuck me harder. It was madness. All of this was madness. Still, I hadn't felt this alive in years.

My romance books had been true. There was something exhilarating about being with a bad boy.

The aura of danger and excitement that encircled him was as intoxicating as it was terrifying. Unlike with other men, there was no line with Maxim. No duty to society's rules. Nothing was off limits. Not tossing me on my dean's desk and fucking me while a classroom of students were in the next room or bending me over a bench and spanking my ass or kidnapping me or even murder. I felt like I was in a speeding car racing around a cliff on a narrow, twisted path. Sometimes we hugged the safety of the mountain, other times the tires teetered on the edge and I could see the ocean below as the waves crashed over the rocks.

It was that knife edge of danger that made the sex so amazing—and so freaking dirty and rough-hot. The way he arrogantly and confidently knew what my body wanted—what it needed—despite my protests. What normal man could compete with that balls-to-the-wall swagger? It was like Maxim had stepped straight out of a book or movie. This whole situation felt like that. Everything from the moment I had met him felt unreal. The problem was this bad boy fantasy had real-world consequences. It wasn't my imagination that Dylan's uncle was killed today, possibly by the very man I'd just had sex with.

And now he was trying to teach me how to fire a gun for my own protection.

We were inside one of the shooting stalls, located right next to the wood-paneled room. There was a counter flanked by two bulletproof glass brass deflector panels. According to Maxim, it was to prevent the hot metal bullet chambers from flying into the lane next to mine. As well as any bullets, should there be an errant shot or ricochet. We faced a long narrow corridor covered in dark gray panels. At the end was a large piece of white paper with the silhouette of a man's torso on it.

I was holding another Glock, but this one was much

smaller than the one he had forced into my hand earlier. It was more lightweight and looked like I could just pop it into my purse. That is, if I had my purse. I had left it behind with my phone when Maxim dragged me out of school today. That was another way this whole thing had an unreal feel to it. Without my phone, I was disconnected from the rest of the world. My entire world was now Maxim. He assured me Dylan was fine and I would actually see her tomorrow, but until then, it would just be me and him.

Once again, that strange mixture of fear and excitement twisted and curled in the pit of my stomach.

Maxim took the gun from my hand. He pulled out the magazine and filled it with bullets before clicking it back into place and handing it to me. "Now that the gun is loaded, you want to pull back on the slide."

I pinched the back of the gun with my thumb and forefinger and pulled. It slid more easily than I thought it would. A small rectangular chamber opened up and I watched as a brass bullet popped into place before the slide clicked back into position.

Maxim stepped behind me. "Now remember what I said about your stance. Feet apart. Hips straight. Put your finger on the trigger, but don't press it yet."

I placed my finger on the trigger.

"Good girl. Now you just want to press gently on the trigger with steady, even pressure. If you pull too hard, the gun will jolt to the right. If you're too tense, it will jump to the left. Just relax and press it when you are ready."

He placed the black earmuffs over my ears. I was already wearing a pair of tinted safety glasses. Staring straight ahead, I closed one eye to focus on the target. I inhaled and held my breath as I pressed the trigger.

The bullet bounced off the floor, completely missing the target.

Maxim stepped close. He pulled one of the earmuffs off my ear. "That's good for a first shot. What happened is your wrist broke downward, so the shot went low. This time, focus on keeping your wrist straight and don't hold your breath."

"I wasn't holding my breath!"

He stroked my cheek. "Yes, baby, you were. You also bit your lip as you concentrated. It was adorable, but not great for accuracy. This time, inhale and then pull the trigger as you exhale."

I adjusted my feet and raised the gun a second time. This time I inhaled… held my breath for a second… then exhaled just as I pulled the trigger. I hit the target square in the chest.

I pulled the earmuffs off my ears to rest around my neck. "Holy shit! I hit it! I hit it!" I bounced up and down and threw myself into Maxim's arms.

He hugged me tight. As I continued to bounce with excitement, he reached behind him and took the gun from my hand. "Don't forget, it's still loaded."

I was too excited to notice. "I can't believe I hit the target on my second try."

He brushed the curls away from my face. "I can. You're a natural. I'm very proud of you."

I stilled as my stomach did a somersault. A warm glow started deep within my belly at his praise. It shouldn't matter, but it did. I was pleased that I had made him proud.

"Now let's see if you can do it again."

He squared my hips up and stepped behind me. He wrapped his arm around my waist and pulled me close. I turned to look at him over my shoulder. "You know, this is kind of distracting."

He pushed my hair aside and nuzzled my neck. "Good. You won't always have time to shoot under perfect conditions. A minor distraction will teach you to concentrate."

I pulled the earmuffs back into place and adjusted my safety goggles.

He handed me the gun, then placed his hand just below my right breast, cupping my ribs.

Under the guise of perfecting my stance, I wiggled my hips against his crotch.

He reached up and pinched my nipple. "Behave, or I'll show you another way I can use that gun in your hand."

My mouth dropped open. "You don't mean... you couldn't... you wouldn't..."

He sank his teeth into my earlobe before flicking it with his tongue. "I do mean. I could. And I will one day."

"But... but..." I couldn't form any words. I was speechless as the image of what he was implying made my cheeks burn.

He slipped his hand to cup me between my legs. The thin fabric of my yoga pants was no protection against the stimulating warmth of his hand. His other hand reached up to pinch my left nipple again. "You think the only way you can come is from my cock or my tongue? I'll show you what a rush it is to face death. I'll fuck you with my gun barrel while I suck on these gorgeous tits of yours. I'll make my dirty girl scream my name."

My knees almost buckled. I had to lean up against him to keep myself upright.

Fuck, that was dirty sexy hot.

And there was definitely something seriously wrong with me for even thinking so.

Deciding it was safer to fire a deadly weapon than to continue along this line of conversation, I faced forward and raised my arms. Like he had taught me, I inhaled, then exhaled and fired. I hit the target again.

Maxim would not let me rest until I had emptied four magazines full of bullets. We went through three targets. By the end, I was hitting the silhouette in center mass as well as a few head shots.

Maxim then had me fire a similar small revolver.

He showed me how to load it. "This is the gun I want you to carry around with you."

I held up my hand. "Wait. You want me to carry a gun? Like all the time?"

"Yes. Keep it in your purse. I prefer the Glock, but the Smith & Wesson revolver is a better option since you can fire one through the fabric of your purse without it jamming." He handed the gun back to me. "I'll get a custom one made for you later, but this will do for now."

"Don't I need to go through a background check or take a class or get a permit or something?"

He tapped the edge of my nose with his finger. "You're adorable. No. It's handled. Now square up your hips and let's practice with the revolver."

I was fairly certain his idea of handled wasn't exactly legal, but I didn't want to fight. I was actually starting to relax a little in his presence, and it was nice. He still wasn't boyfriend material by any means and there was no way this was going anywhere, but maybe for now I could just stop fighting it and return to my original idea of just having fun with him.

Fun that apparently required me to carry a gun for my protection.

You know, normal dating stuff.

Once we were done, Maxim led me back into the other room to get a gun case and some more ammunition. While he gathered up the items, I stared at the workbench and thought about all that had transpired in the last few hours. My gaze caught on his gun.

Would I have pulled the trigger?

Of course not. At least I didn't think I would have.

Besides, it wasn't like he handed me a loaded gun. It was just a test. I was sure if I had pulled the trigger, nothing would have happened. He probably would have laughed and told me the safety had been on… or taken me over his knee and spanked my ass raw as punishment for calling his bluff and trying to kill him.

Curious, I bit my lip. Keeping my gaze on his gun, I asked, "What would you have done if I had actually pulled the trigger?"

Maxim shrugged. "Died."

"I'm serious."

"So am I."

I huffed. "No, you're not. I knew it. There weren't any bullets in it. Right? You were never in any real danger."

Maxim raised a single eyebrow. Strolling toward me, he picked up the gun and headed straight back to the shooting stall. I followed in his wake.

Without hesitating, he pulled back the slide and emptied the entire magazine into the target. It shredded the paper as he blew away the silhouette's head. The smell of sulfur and metal grease permeated the air as a thin cloud of smoke rose up around us.

He clicked a button and the magazine dropped to the counter. He then picked up a fresh magazine and reloaded the gun before tucking it into the holster behind his back.

My jaw dropped open. "It was loaded!"

He nodded.

I threw my arms up into the air. "It was loaded? As in *loaded*! As in, if I had pulled the trigger, you would have freaking *died*! I could have *killed* you!"

He wrapped his hand around the back of my neck and pulled me in close for a quick hard kiss on the lips. "Don't worry, *moya malen'kaya iskra*. I'm not that easy to get rid of."

CHAPTER 18

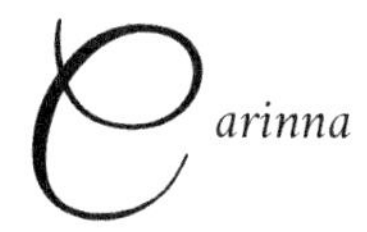*arinna*

It was dark by the time we pulled up to my apartment building. As I reached to unbuckle my seat belt, I saw Maxim do the same. "I don't suppose you're just going to walk me to the door."

He raised an eyebrow, then got out of the car without saying a word. He circled around and opened my door and helped me out before popping the trunk and pulling out a black duffle bag. He placed a hand on my lower back as we walked toward my building.

"You seem like you're a pretty rich guy. Why aren't you staying at a hotel or something?"

He held open the outside door for me. "I hate hotels."

"So that's what this is all about? You're with me for a free place to crash because you don't like hotels?" I asked as I walked down the corridor to my apartment.

"Not dislike. Hate. The idea of sleeping in a bed hundreds,

if not thousands, of other men have slept in does not appeal to me."

I raised an eyebrow and flashed him a cheeky grin. "How do you know that isn't the case with my bed?"

Dropping his duffle bag, he pressed me against the wall just outside my apartment. He placed his forearms on either side of my head, caging me in. "If I thought that for one second, *moya malen'kaya iskra,* I would be very busy killing every man on that list. Besides, you forget. I've been inside that tight pussy of yours. It's all highway."

My brow furrowed. "All highway?"

"Like a car, it's only been driven on the easy highway streets. No off-roading or rough treatment."

"Not until you came along," I mumbled as I crossed my arms under my chest. "I'm not sure I enjoy being compared to a car."

He backed up a step and raised his arm in the air as he covered his heart with his other hand. *"Mogu ya sravnit' tebya letnim dnom? Ty mileye i ravneye: Burnyye vetera tryasut lyubimyye mayskiye pochki i leto slishkom korotkoye."*

Before I could ask him what he was saying, he leaned over me, pressing his hips into mine. His lips caressed my mouth as he recited Shakespeare's Sonnet Eighteen. "Shall I compare thee to a summer's day? Thou art more lovely and more temperate: Rough winds do shake the darling buds of May, And summer's lease hath all too short a date."

I rolled my eyes. "Great, a Russian gangster who quotes Shakespeare. Every girl's dream boyfriend."

Maxim laughed as he picked up his duffle bag and turned to unlock the door.

I pressed my palms to my hips and then looked around me as if my backpack and purse would magically appear. "Oh, no! I left my things at the school. We have to go back. My phone's in there. Maybe the night janitor will let us in."

Maxim opened the door with the key he took from me earlier and gestured for me to walk inside. "It is being taken care of."

"What does that mean?"

"That means I called one of my men and they are in the process of getting your things from the school."

"But it's locked. How will they get in?"

Maxim just smiled as he tossed his duffle bag on the floor near my sofa and headed to the refrigerator. "Do not ask questions you don't want to know the answers to."

The same thing had happened with my car. He must have a team of ninja lock pickers around the city, like some anti-Batman.

Before Maxim, the only thing in my fridge was some old Chinese food and butter for baking, occasionally a container of buttermilk. Now it was filled with groceries and alcohol.

He pulled out a beer for himself and grabbed a fresh bottle of white wine for me. He reached into the cabinet for a wineglass and then the utensil drawer for the wine opener and poured me a glass. I noticed he didn't have to search around. He knew precisely where everything was kept. I didn't know whether to feel comforted by that or completely freaked out.

I stopped with the glass half raised to my mouth. "How did you know I liked white wine?"

His beer can had a bunch of Russian Cyrillic writing on it. I did not know where a person would even find Russian beer in Chicago. I glanced behind him and saw my wine bottle was the type I usually purchased for myself.

He took a long draw off his can of beer as he leaned against the kitchen counter. "Your social media accounts. There are photos of you drinking only white wine or margaritas. I also noticed the kind you liked from a photo taken inside this kitchen."

I took another sip of wine to cover my nervousness. "You know, in America, we would consider it super creepy to admit you had stalked a prospective date on social media."

"Are you saying no one looks at a date's social media in America?"

I laughed. "Oh, hell, no, especially the women. We'd practically know the guy's Social Security number and his mother's maiden name before he picked us up for our first date."

Maxim shrugged. "Then what is the problem?"

The problem was he didn't just look at my social media. He acted on the information very thoughtfully by buying some of my favorite foods and wine. The problem was it made him look like boyfriend material, which I already knew he most certainly was not. The problem was it showed him to be charming and sweet instead of the demanding and dangerous man I knew him to be.

"There's no problem exactly. It's just that Americans don't admit to stalking each other's social media. We politely pretend to learn those things about the person on the date."

"So you lie. You're mad because I'm being honest."

"No, not exactly." I let out a frustrated sigh. "You're missing my point."

He set his beer can down and approached me. He placed his finger under my chin and lifted my gaze to his. "The more important things you cannot learn from social media." He skimmed his lips over my cheek to my ear. "Like the cute sound you make when my tongue piercing flicks your clit. Or how you rise on your toes when I spank your adorable ass or when you…"

My cheeks flamed. I stepped away and downed the rest of my wine. "I get your point."

Before he could respond, there was a knock on my door. As I moved to answer, Maxim raised his hand to stop me. He pulled out his gun and approached the door.

My heart stopped. I moved around to place the kitchen island between me and the door as I looked around for where I'd left my selfie stick weapon.

"*Eto ya,* boss," came a muffled voice through the door.

Maxim put his gun on the counter and opened the door. There was a quick conversation in Russian, then he closed and locked it. He turned and tossed my backpack and purse onto the table.

I pounced on both. Pulling out my phone, I was grateful it still had at least a small charge. I scrolled through the texts. There was a quick one from Dylan letting me know she was okay and we'd talk tomorrow, and then another from my boss.

"I have to go," I announced as I tossed my phone down and turned to go into my bedroom.

Maxim grabbed me by the upper arm. "You're not going anywhere."

I shook him off and headed into the bedroom. "Yes, I am. My boss texted. He needs me to work."

Maxim followed me. "I thought you said I got you fired."

I shrugged as I reached into my bureau to pull out a pair of dark jeans and a black lace top. "Obviously, you've never worked in the hospitality industry before. Everyone's always fired until the next person on the schedule pulls a 'no call no show' and they need you to cover a shift. Then all is forgiven."

I kicked off my sneakers and headed toward the bathroom door.

Maxim placed his arm across the threshold and blocked my path. "No."

"What do you mean, no?"

"Just what I said, no."

"You know I'm getting really tired of hearing you say that word."

"Then stop trying to test my authority. I will not have you working at that place, or anywhere else for that matter."

I blinked several times as my mouth dropped open. "Your authority? *Your authority?* What is this, the 1950s? You don't have any authority over me."

He looked down at me. "I believe I have already proven the many ways I do."

I backed away a few steps, holding my clothes close to my chest as if they were a protective shield. "Listen, the last twenty-four hours have been crazy and I'll definitely never forget them, but I have to get back to reality and the reality is that I have bills to pay. Rent. Tuition. My parents."

He frowned. "What do you mean, your parents?"

I waved away his question. "Never mind that. The point is, I have bills and for that I need money and in order to get money I have to work."

Maxim stormed out of the bedroom.

Holy shit. That had worked? I didn't think he'd back down, but apparently reminding him that some of us lived in the real world and not some *Goodfellas* movie had gotten through to him.

Maxim quickly returned. In his hand was a fat roll of American currency. All hundreds, from the look of it. He tore off the rubber band holding the roll in place and started counting off bills. "How much do you want? One thousand? Two? Five? What do you need? It's yours."

The temptation to take him up on his offer rose deep inside of me. Five thousand dollars would pay my rent for a few months and allow me to focus on school. I ruthlessly pushed the thought aside. Just like Dylan, I still had my pride, and I had no intention of taking any money from him.

I tossed the clothes I was holding to the floor as I placed my fists on my hips. "Are you calling me a whore?"

Maxim stopped counting off bills. His head tilted to the

right as his eyes narrowed. I had already learned that was a warning sign, but I was too angry to care.

"Is that what you think? That you can just toss money at me to get your way as if I were nothing better than a whore?"

He tossed the heavy roll of cash onto my nightstand, the symbolism of which made this whole thing way worse. "What would you call a woman who displays her tits to strange men for tips?"

With a shriek of rage, I picked up a small figurine of a ballerina from on top of my bureau and threw it at him. "It's called being a bartender, you asshole, not a fucking whore!"

Maxim ducked to one side. The figurine shattered against the wall. Glaring at me from across the room, he pulled off his shirt, exposing his massive, tattooed chest and piercings. Somehow it managed to make him look bigger and even more fierce. What the hell had I just done?

He reached down and unbuckled his belt. He bent it in half, fisted both ends, and snapped it together. The crack of the hard leather reverberated around the room.

I picked up a Chicago-themed mug I kept hair ties in and chucked it at him. "Get out!"

He circled around the bed. "I've told you before, I'm not going anywhere."

In desperation, I threw my hairbrush at him. The pink plastic brush bounced off his chest.

"You think you can offer me money and call me a whore and—"

He stalked around to my side of the bed as he unbuttoned the top button of his pants. "You *are* my little whore. A dirty girl who likes to pick fights, so she doesn't have to be ashamed of liking rough sex."

The truth of his words hit me like a punch to the stomach. It was easier to fuck and fight with him than to admit I liked the violent way he manhandled me. I even liked the dirty, degrading way he talked to me while he was fucking me. It was raw and nasty and so wrong, but there was no denying it was the best mind-blowing sex of my life. Still, that didn't mean I was going to sacrifice my pride for a few good orgasms.

He cornered me between the wall and the bed, blocking the only exit. With flight not possible, I had no other option. I flew at him with my fists raised. "Fuck you!"

CHAPTER 19

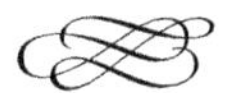

axim

IF A FIGHT WAS what she wanted, what she needed, then I would give her a fight.

I grabbed her wrist and spun her around, pinning her body to mine from behind. I wrapped my arm around her shoulders, securing her. Leaning down, I whispered harshly into her ear, “I'm going to fuck you so hard you'll worship me as your new god.”

“Never,” she ground out as she struggled against my grasp.

“I'll have you on your knees, begging for my cock.”

Carinna sank her teeth into my forearm. Deep. I could feel the moment she broke skin. With a growl, I released my grasp. Spinning her to face me, I grabbed her by the throat, just under her jaw. “Careful, babygirl. I bite back.”

I thrust my arm out, shoving her onto the bed. She fell backward, but quickly scrambled to her hands and knees.

She crawled off the bed and launched herself at the bedroom door. I stepped onto the center of the bed and jumped down, landing behind her. Reaching up, I flattened my palm against the door's edge and slammed it shut before she could fully open it.

Carinna rattled the doorknob, then threw a glare over her shoulder. Her usually brown eyes were bright and golden with fear and lust. "Open the door."

"No."

"Open the fucking door Maxim."

"No."

She rattled the doorknob again, pulling on it with all her strength. My palm kept it closed.

She threw her elbow back, catching me in the stomach.

I wrapped my arm around her waist and pulled her away from the door. Using my free hand, I gripped the collar of her T-shirt and tore. The flimsy material shredded. Ignoring her outraged shrieks, I snapped the plastic front clasp on her bra. As Carinna pulled away from me, I fisted the material of her T-shirt and bra behind her back, pulling it down her arms and off her body.

She spun to face me, her arms only partially covering her breasts. The soft pink of her areolas peeked out above her arms.

I licked my lips. "First thing tomorrow, I'm getting your nipples pierced."

Her eyes widened to saucers.

I smiled. "I'm going to have them attach a long chain that links to my cock ring."

She backed away a few steps.

I followed. "You will be forced to crawl on your knees and follow my cock around."

"I'll see you in hell first," she spit out as she threw another fragile piece of porcelain at me.

This one bounced off my upper arm and fell to the floor without breaking. I kicked it aside as I continued to stalk her around the room. When I had her cornered, I reached out and snatched her body to mine. I fisted her hair and pulled her head back, forcing her gaze to clash with mine. "Don't you know, babygirl? I'm the devil. Hell is wherever I am."

With that, I claimed her mouth, swallowing her outraged cries.

I pinned her against the wall. Opening her legs, I pushed my hips into hers as my tongue shoved past her resisting lips. When a kiss was not enough to appease my already painfully hard cock, I reached around her body, lifted her high and carried her to the bed. This time, when I tossed her into the center, my body followed, crushing her beneath my substantial weight. I nudged her thighs open with my own and ground my cock against her core.

I lifted my head and stared down into her defiant eyes. "Open your mouth."

Her lips thinned as she snapped them tightly closed.

I lifted my hand to her jaw and pushed the tips of my fingers into her cheeks to force her mouth open. "I said, open your mouth, whore."

She bared her teeth and hissed at me. My gorgeous little spitfire. *Moya malen'kaya iskra.*

I pushed two fingers past her teeth. Flattening her tongue, I shoved them in deep.

Carinna gagged and choked.

"Suck on my fingers. Soon it will be my cock."

I thrust a third finger into her mouth, splaying them open. Enjoying how her pink lips stretched to accommodate them as I pushed them in deep.

Her shoulders hunched as she gagged a second time.

Taking pity on her, I removed my hand and used my wet fingers to tease her nipples. They glistened with her spit when I stretched out my tongue to lick them further. I teased the flesh till a moan was wrenched from her body as her back arched.

Leaning upward, I pulled her head against my chest. "I want your tongue on my nipples."

I heard her teeth clatter against the metal barbell piercing that went across my nipple as well as the additional piercings through my pectoral muscles. As she dutifully licked and laved, I moved my hand to between her legs. Slipping under her yoga pants, I teased her cunt. My fingers easily slipped inside her tight, wet sheath.

Pulling my fingers free, I tilted her head back, away from my chest. I slid my wet fingertips across her full bottom lip. "Proof you love being treated like my dirty little whore."

Carinna moaned as her eyes slid closed.

I shook her. "Open your eyes."

She obeyed.

"Lick your lips. I want you to taste your own arousal."

The tip of her cute tongue flicked out to trace her bottom lip.

"Good girl."

Leaving her warmth, I stood at the end of the bed. Keeping my heated gaze trained on her, I kicked off my shoes and lowered the zipper on my pants. "Take off your clothes."

Carinna's eyes were half open as her head lolled to one side. Her hands reached for the waistband of her yoga pants and panties. She pulled them down to her knees. She then lifted her legs, giving me a glimpse of her ass as she pulled them over her calves and flung them to the side.

I kicked my pants free and joined her on the bed.

She placed a restraining hand on my chest. "Please, don't do this. I can't. I'm too sore."

Once again, I traced her kiss-swollen lips with my fingertips. "Don't worry, baby. I'm not fucking that hole."

As realization dawned, she shook her head as she tried to scamper back from me on the bed. I grabbed her hips, flipped her over, and forced her onto her hands and knees. I placed a restraining hand on the back of her head, pushing down until she kissed the bedcovers.

She cried out, "No! I've never done that!"

Scanning her bureau top for something I could use as lube, I reached for a small jar of petroleum jelly. Popping off the lid, I scooped a generous amount onto my fingers. I then fisted my cock, spreading it along the shaft. I scooped up an additional amount and commanded, "Hold open your ass cheeks."

The bedcovers muffled her refusal.

With my free hand, I spanked her ass several times. Bright red handprints glowed on her pale skin. Carinna cried out and bucked her hips forward. I pulled her back onto her hands and knees and once again commanded, "Open your ass cheeks or I swear to God, baby, I'll fuck you raw with no lube at all."

Sniffling, her shaking arms reached out and pulled her cheeks open.

"Wider," I barked.

She obeyed.

Her tiny little anus winked at me as I pressed two fingertips to the hole. Her skin glistened as the petroleum jelly melted. I caressed the soft ridges as I teased her dark entrance with the tip of my finger. I pushed in and out, gently opening her. Once she was more accustomed to this, I would be able to bend her over and take her hard and fast, but for this first time, I needed to be careful… at least at first. I continued to push in one finger for a few minutes before adding a second one, pushing in to the first knuckle.

Carinna whimpered but stayed still.

"Good girl," I softly crooned. "One more finger."

"No, please…"

"Soon you'll be taking my cock, which, trust me, baby, is a great deal wider than a few fingers," I warned.

I pulled free and dipped my fingers back into the jar. This time, I opened her further with three fingers to the knuckle. I twisted back and forth, watching as her dark pink skin whitened from the pressure.

When I pulled free, her tiny hole didn't immediately contract.

It was time.

I rose up on my knees and fisted my cock. I teased her sensitive entrance with the ring and ball from my piercing. Swirling the head around her hole, coating it further in the warm, melted petroleum jelly.

Finally, I pushed.

Her body clenched, barring my entrance as she released her grip on her cheeks.

I spanked her again, before using my own hands to spread her open wide.

Using my hips, I pushed forward a second time, increasing the pressure. The feel of her punishment-heated skin against my own made my cock lengthen and thicken even further.

Her tiny hole relented as the head of my cock slipped inside. The tight ring of muscle then closed around the top of my shaft. I threw my head back and groaned, summoning every ounce of restraint in my body not to pound into her without mercy.

Her body shifted as she swallowed a sob.

Knowing going any more slowly would only prolong the pain, I gripped her hips and thrust.

Carinna shrieked as she tried to fall forward. My grasp on her body wouldn't allow her. I pulled back my hips and thrust again.

"Please, go slower!"

"No," I responded through clenched teeth.

Taking her anal virginity was quite possibly the single most glorious sexual experience of my life. She was so fucking tight and the idea that I was the first—and if I had my way, the only—man to experience her amazing body this way sent a wave of possessive pleasure coursing through my limbs.

I pulled back and thrust forward a third time, watching as her tiny hole stretched around the thick base of my cock.

Carinna fisted the bedcovers as her whole body trembled and squirmed. "Please!" she begged.

I thrust again. Her hole was opening, accepting my body deep within her own.

As my thrusts took on a slow and deep rhythm, I reached around her hip to tease her clit with my hand.

Carinna's body bucked the moment I touched her sweet pussy.

"That's it, baby. Tell me you like this. Tell me you enjoy having my cock deep in your ass."

I pinched her clit, feeling her get even wetter.

I timed the thrusts of my cock in her ass to the strokes of my fingertips on her clit. "Come on, baby. Tell me you're my dirty girl."

A tremor rippled over her body as goosebumps skittered over her flesh. "Oh, God! I am! I am!"

Her body opened up further. As her hole relaxed, I thrust harder. "Say it," I demanded. "Say you're my dirty little whore who likes her ass fucked."

She threw her head back as she came. "I'm your dirty little whore, Maxim. I'm yours," she breathed.

With her release, her body clenched down hard on my cock, sending a glorious spasm up my shaft and straight to my balls.

And with that, I lost all restraint.

Slapping her ass, I twisted my hand into her hair and pounded into her body as if the very hounds of hell were on my heels. I was a brutal beast, ruthlessly using her body for my own pleasure. I trained my gaze on her ass, watching as my cock disappeared into her body over and over again. The pressure of my release twisted my stomach until my abdominal muscles tightened and clenched.

With a roar, I released a hot stream of come deep inside her. Even as I came, I continued to thrust, unable to stop despite the sensitive pain that coursed up my shaft. When I finally pulled free, I kept my grip on her hair, wanting to keep her body in place. With my free hand, I pried open her ass cheek, wanting to watch as my thick white come slowly dripped from her now-gaping asshole.

Using my grip, I turned her body around till she was on her knees before me. I gripped my cock. “Now open your mouth.”

CHAPTER 20

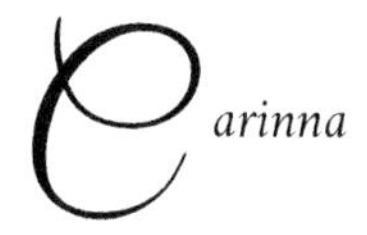

arinna

MAXIM LIFTED my limp and shaking body into his arms and carried me into the bathroom. Resting my head against his chest, I felt the warm metal of his piercings against my cheek as the steady beat of his heart became my only reality.

He had already left the bed once to start the tub faucet and bring me a towel and a small glass half filled with mouthwash.

I couldn't believe I'd done *that*.

Any of *that*.

The whole thing.

The whole dirty sexy raw thing.

And oh, my God, the words that came from my mouth. Had I really begged to be his whore? Had I really happily sucked him off after he—I scrunched my eyes shut tighter.

Humiliation and regret crashed down on me like a bucket of cold water.

The shower curtain had been pushed aside.

He filled the tub with hot water as a fluffy cloud of glistening soap bubbles dripped over the edge. The scent of lavender from my body soap wafted on the steam. I glanced at Maxim. It was odd to have this ferociously masculine and terrifyingly tattooed man standing in the middle of my tiny bathroom, which currently reeked of flowers.

Maxim stepped into the tub and lowered us both down into the hot water. One perk of living in an old building was a large metal tub big enough for two people, not those narrow plastic ones you get in new apartments.

He positioned me between his legs. He then reached for my pink bath pouf, which looked ridiculous in his large inked-up hands. He poured a generous amount of pale pink shimmering body wash onto it and then lathered it up. He ran it over my arms and down my legs.

Pushing my hair aside with his hand, he nuzzled my neck. "Stop."

My brow furrowed. "Stop what?"

"Thinking."

My leg twitched nervously under the water. "I don't know what you're talking about."

He placed a restraining hand on my upper thigh. "Yes, you do, *moya lyubimaya.*"

He moved his hand to cup me between my legs. "Do not turn a fun bedroom game into something that it is not." He moved to caress my belly and breasts.

I took a deep breath and closed my eyes. "This doesn't feel like a game."

His hand stilled.

The only sound in the bathroom was the steady drip from the tub faucet.

His other hand moved up to cup my cheek as he pressed the side of his head to mine. The rough stubble on his jaw scraped my skin as he spoke. "No, babygirl. You are right. This is no game."

I played with the heavy silver band ring around the index finger of the hand that rested on my thigh. I pushed the warm band till it spun around his finger as I studied his hands.

Each knuckle had tiny worn scars in a strange starburst pattern. As if he had repeatedly torn them open from punching something... or someone. Both the back of his hand and his fingers up to the first knuckle were covered in tattoos. Some old and faded, which meant he must have gotten them when he was barely a teenager. They were a compelling mixture of religious idolatry, symbolism, and Cyrillic writing.

His hands were large, powerful, and dangerous. They were both cruel and painful and caressing and comforting. They were like the man himself.

I wish I could say that the man that Maxim was confused me, and mixed up my thinking with competing emotions, but he didn't. He was the most straightforward black and white person I had ever met. He knew what he was, and he didn't apologize for it. He knew what he wanted, and he didn't hesitate to go after it, again with no apology. Throughout this entire roller coaster ride, he had never lied to me. Not once. He had been brutally, startlingly honest about what he wanted from me... from us.

I couldn't be that honest.

I wasn't prepared to face the hidden truth about myself. It was one thing to get aroused from reading a line-pushing sex scene in a book. It was another to live it... to want it. I still couldn't believe the things I had said and done. The things I had begged him to do. My bottom clenched at the remembrance of his cock thrusting in deep. The pain and illicit pleasure were so intense I swore I was going to pass out the moment I came. The thought was terrifying. I didn't want to face this new dark side of my personality. I wanted to go back to the girl who liked to bake French pastries and complain to her friends about the boring missionary sex she got from other men.

What we had just done in my bedroom wasn't just sex. It was primal and violent. If that was where our relationship—if 'relationship' was what you could call this—started, then where did it end? I felt like Alice in Wonderland, tumbling head over heels down a long dark tunnel, uncertain of what was real and what was fiction anymore.

I wanted my innocence back.

I wanted my naivete back.

And that was impossible.

So where did that leave us?

Was he going to turn my entire world topsy-turvy only to leave me after a few weeks? If he even waited that long. Men like Maxim didn't strike me as the monogamous type. Was I going to allow him to open this dark portal into my soul only to leave me feeling empty and hollow, longing for a time before I met him?

I inhaled a shaky breath. "Maxim, I..."

He hugged my body to his. "Shhh, babygirl. Don't say it."

"But I..."

He chuckled mirthlessly. "I already know what you are thinking. Don't put it into words. I beg you."

"We can't keep..."

He pushed my head until it was lying back on his shoulder. He then wrapped his arms tight around my body and slowly rocked us back and forth as he crooned what sounded like a Russian lullaby to me. Water sloshed over the edge of the tub. Maxim's only response was to kick the faucet back on with his foot.

Hot water flowed into the tub. I hadn't known the water

had cooled until I felt the slow progression of the hotter water seep over my calves, my thighs, my stomach, warming me.

His voice was rough, making his Russian accent even heavier, like the low growl of a bear. "Sometimes, we don't know we are cold until we feel the warmth of the sun on our face. I know it's hard to believe when your head is spinning and telling you otherwise, but believe me, babygirl. Sometimes darkness is just darkness. There is no deeper meaning or scary beasts. Just darkness."

"That can't be true. This has to mean something is wrong with me. Something is twisted and broken for me to like… what we just did."

His fingertips traced my collarbone. "I think it means that as a woman, you like a powerful man. You like to challenge him, to fight him. You want him to prove he is strong enough, dominant enough to handle you. A man cannot prove that without fighting for you. Fighting for the honor of a place between those gorgeous thighs of yours."

"You make it sound like some chivalric battle from some fairy tale."

"And why shouldn't it be? Why shouldn't I be the dark knight who wins the fair maiden's charms?"

I captured his hand and held it over my heart. "Because you're supposed to be the villain."

He ran his lips over the outer edge of my ear before flicking my earlobe, then gently biting it. "What your fairy tales never tell you is that often, *moya lyubimaya,* it is the villain who wins, because it is the villain who is willing to fight, no matter the cost, for what he wants."

I sighed as I once more rested my head in the crook of his shoulder. "So am I the fair maiden or the whore in this story?"

He chuckled as he softly pinched my nipple. "Both. It is

why I find you so beautiful and so fascinating. You, my Carinna Giovanna Russo, are a hard woman to resist."

"And you, Maxim Konatantinovich Miloslavsky, are a dangerous man to know."

"No, not dangerous for you, never for you."

"So what happens now? Am I supposed to just take your hand and skip down into the ever-deepening darkness?"

"No."

My heart skipped a beat. Was he finally admitting this was all just a passing heat of the moment thing and he was leaving? Why did the thought of never seeing him again terrify me more than what would happen to my soul if he stayed? "There's your favorite word again."

He chuckled. "What I meant to say was no, let's not talk about tomorrow. Let's only talk about right now."

I nodded. "Okay, then. What happens right now?"

He pulled my face to the side and gave me a hard kiss on the lips. "Right now, we get some food. I'm starving."

I laughed and splashed him with the soapy water.

CHAPTER 21

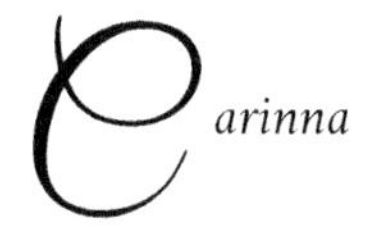

arinna

Maxim pulled away from the curb after making sure I was buckled in. "Let's go over the rules one more time."

I let out a dramatic sigh. "We've been over this twice already!"

"Carinna."

I let out another dramatic sigh. "Fine! Under no circumstances am I to leave the hotel room until you come to get me. If I need something the hotel can provide, I'm to talk to the guard, not the hotel staff. I'm to call you immediately if there are any issues."

Maxim was taking me to see Dylan. I hadn't seen or talked to her since the morning she found all that cash and brought these Russians crashing into our world. Right now she was staying at some super swanky private hotel with Ivan. I couldn't wait to give her a big hug and to make sure she was okay after what happened with her uncle.

Wait.

I turned to Maxim. "Does Dylan know about her uncle?"

"Does she know he was a piece of shit bastard who liked to beat on women? Yes, I'm pretty sure she knows that," responded Maxim sardonically.

I slapped him playfully on the shoulder. "You know what I mean. Does she know... does she know you and your friends *killed him*?" I said the last two words in a whisper after glancing around the interior of the car.

Keeping his eyes on the traffic, Maxim leaned over closer to me. "Why are you whispering?" he asked in a loud stage whisper.

Realizing how silly I was being since we were obviously the only two people in the car, I laughed. "Sorry, I'm still getting the hang of the mafia wife stuff." My cheeks flamed hot as I stammered, "Not that I'm your wife. Or that I want to be your wife. I mean, I'm not even your girlfriend. I just said mafia wife because that's what they are in the movies. Not because I want to be your wife or anything. That would be stupid. We've only known one another for two freaking days. We're not even dating. I don't know why I said mafia wife. I didn't mean it that way. It's really just an expression, an American turn of phrase, it means nothing."

Maxim placed his large hand over mine, which were twisting the button on my coat in my nervousness. "*Moya malen'kaya iskra,* I know what you meant."

I let out the breath I was holding and raised my travel mug to my lips.

Maxim winked at me. "Although Carinna Giovanna Miloslavskaya does have a nice ring to it."

I choked on my coffee. "You're not serious."

Maxim shrugged. "Do not worry, *moya lyubimaya.* I have no afternoon plans to drag you by your hair into a dark cave with a priest waiting there to pronounce marriage vows over us."

"Well, that's good. Because I already had afternoon plans," I responded sarcastically, even as I imagined how devilishly handsome he'd look in a tuxedo.

Maxim plucked the coffee mug from my hand and took a sip, then handed it back to me. "I make no promises about my plans for tomorrow afternoon."

"I can never tell if you're kidding or not."

We pulled up to a stoplight. Maxim turned the full weight of his intense emerald gaze on me. "I will make it easy on you, babygirl. I rarely kid."

I blinked.

We pulled up to the hotel, sparing me from having to respond.

Maxim walked me up to the room. As we strolled down the hallway, I could hear female voices.

"That must be Mary and Emma. They are the wives of two of my friends. Ivan mentioned they were also coming over," said Maxim.

I hid my disappointment. It would have been nice to meet with Dylan alone. There was no way I could tell her everything I wanted to discuss in front of two strangers. Although perhaps that was for the best; the last thing Dylan needed right now was for me to burden her with my confused feelings for Maxim.

Maxim stopped just out of view of the door. "Remember to behave yourself," he admonished as he tapped the edge of my nose.

I pouted. "I'm not a child, you know."

He smirked. "No, but I'll take you over my knee and spank you like one if I find out you stepped out of line."

At my outraged gasp, he gave me a peck on the cheek and strolled away, laughing.

* * *

"CARINNA!" screamed Dylan as she launched herself at me.

We hugged each other tight. "Oh, my God, I was so worried," she said. At first, I was confused, then I remembered how Maxim had kidnapped me and had taken me to the warehouse. Damn, that felt like years ago instead of yesterday. Dylan probably knew they had snatched me up for my protection, but I wasn't sure what she knew beyond that.

I played dumb, at least while we were in front of strangers. I pointed to her black eye. "Did Ivan do that?" Part of me wanted to be reassured he hadn't done it. For all I knew, the talk of Dylan's uncle giving her a black eye could have been a lie to cover up Ivan's violence. I needed to hear it straight from Dylan.

"No! No, it was my Uncle Frank."

I paused and bit my lip. Fuck. Whenever she talked about her family, or I talked about mine, we always jokingly said we'd kill the person to ease the tension. I did not know for absolutely certain if Dylan knew her uncle was really dead. Fuck. Fuck. Fuck. What do I say? Weakly, I responded, "I'll kill him."

One of the women I later learned was Mary chimed in as she flounced down on the sofa, "Too late. Ivan already took care of that."

I looked at Dylan to see her reaction to such a casual admission that the man she was staying with at this hotel had killed her uncle.

She leaned in and whispered, "I'll tell you later."

The pregnant one, Emma, sat down too. "I'm starving. Mary, when is the food coming?"

Before Mary could answer, there was a knock on the door. The guard opened it. "Room service is here."

"Voila!" said Mary as she popped up to greet the hotel

staff member. "I ordered from their afternoon tea menu."

The room service attendant wheeled in a cart with several three-tiered silver trays filled with tiny sandwiches and little cakes and cookies. I surveyed the selection and frowned. It was obvious this fancy hotel didn't have a pastry chef on staff. I could tell from the crumbly rounded edges and the dull gleam on the macarons that most of this stuff was store bought and probably previously frozen.

No longer interested in the pastries, I headed over to the racks of clothes as Emma and Mary poured cups of tea. "Shut. Up. Dylan, are these all yours?"

"No," Dylan said as Mary and Emma both said, "Yes."

"Don't be mad. Ivan texted and asked what I thought your size was and what clothes you'd like," admitted Mary.

Emma added, "Then Mary brought me in on a group chat and... well... we may have gone a little overboard with our suggestions."

"A little?" Dylan asked incredulously. "Do you see all the clothes that man bought?"

Emma shrugged. "How were we supposed to know he'd buy *everything* we mentioned?"

Mary bit into a green macaron. "Although in all fairness, knowing how our men go overboard, we probably should have known."

I unzipped the Gucci garment bag and rifled through the dresses. "Oh, sweetie. You need to keep this man and I'm not just saying that because we're the same size."

Emma picked up her teacup. "Let's have a fashion show! I need to live vicariously."

Dylan objected. "No. There will be no fashion show. I'm not keeping any of these clothes or the jewels."

Mary sat up straighter. "Jewels? What jewels? Oh! Did he give you those pearls?"

Dylan reached for the strands. "Yes, but I'm not keeping

them."

Emma nodded sagely. "We understand." She gestured to Mary. "We both tried to refuse extravagant jewelry gifts from our men early on too."

Dylan leaned forward in her seat. "What did they say when you gave the gifts back?"

Emma rolled up her sweater sleeve to expose an outrageously gorgeous diamond bracelet as Mary pulled her black cardigan sweater off to expose a diamond brooch in the shape of a panther.

Mary tilted her head to the side. "What do you think?"

Dylan frowned. "Honestly, no offense to either of you, but I don't know how you put up with these Russian men. They are so arrogant and bossy and demanding—"

I cut her off, warming up to the topic as I thought of Maxim. "And brutish and stubborn and demanding."

"I already said demanding."

I crossed my arms over my chest. "It bore repeating."

Mary lifted the basket of muffins and offered them to me. I selected a blueberry one and tore into it with more aggression than was necessary for a small pastry.

Mary said, "I guess I don't need to ask if you enjoyed your time with Maxim."

I scoffed. "The man is a terror. He should be locked up in a cage like a wild animal."

Dylan leaned over and touched my knee. "I'm so sorry. It was all my fault. I guess Ivan was worried about your safety after they found my apartment trashed."

Mary patted Dylan on the shoulder. "Hold on." She looked at me and raised an eyebrow. "And?"

I blushed and tore off another piece of muffin. "And what?"

Mary's lips quirked. "And?"

I huffed as my cheeks flamed. There was no way I was

going to admit to these women or even to Dylan that I had already played the whore for Maxim several times, despite only knowing him for two days. "And… maybe… he's also kind of charming in a rough-around-the-edges sort of way and a good kisser."

Kissing. Yuuupppp… that's all we did. I'll tell Dylan the truth later when we're alone.

Mary clapped. "I knew it!"

Emma shook her head. "Face it, ladies. It's hard to resist a Russian man, especially when they growl at you in that sexy accent of theirs."

"Well, I have every intention of resisting Ivan," said Dylan.

Emma's brow wrinkled. "Why? He seems like such a teddy bear."

"A teddy bear? Have you met the man?"

"Yeah, he brought McDonald's to our house a few days ago. He seemed nice."

Mary rolled her eyes. "You think everyone is nice."

Emma winked and quoted Shakespeare. "The robbed that smiles, steals something from the thief."

Dylan shook her head. "Isn't that from Othello? The guy who kills his wife in a fit of jealousy?"

Emma frowned. "True, but the sentiment is the same."

Dylan pushed a yellow macaron around her plate. "Doesn't it bother you? The fact that they're criminals?"

Mary shrugged. "It did at first, but then you just start to see past that and start seeing them for the men they are despite it. They are fiercely loyal, and supportive, and caring. From what I've heard about your family, you had as crappy of a childhood as I did, so I can tell you, it's nice knowing I have over six feet of raging muscle in my corner willing to fight for me and protect me."

Her words hit closer to the truth than I would like to admit.

CHAPTER 22

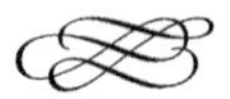

Maxim

I SLAMMED the car door shut and headed toward the back of the loading dock area. Calling out as I walked, "I know. I'm late. I had to pick Carinna up at the hotel and drop her off at pastry class first."

Dimitri, Vaska, Ivan, and Gregor all exchanged looks before bursting into laughter.

Vaska gestured toward me with his McDonald's coffee cup. "Don't forget about the bake sale on Friday."

Dimitri slapped me on the back. "So are you still driving the Mercedes-Benz, or did you trade it in for a station wagon? I hear the Volvo V90 is a nice one."

I flipped him my middle finger.

Gregor held up his hands. "Hey, leave the poor bastard alone."

I nodded toward him. "Thank you, Gregor."

Gregor then added, "He's probably stressed enough doing

the laundry and worrying about dinner."

They all laughed.

I smirked. "Go ahead and laugh it up." I pointed to Vaska. "Thanks to your wife's interesting taste in decor, you live in a vampire's den now." I then pointed to Gregor. "And you have baby vomit on your suit."

Gregor looked at his shoulder. He then grabbed some napkins from their pile of McDonald's take away bags and wiped at the spot. "Why the fuck didn't you two tell me?" he asked, casting accusing glances at Dimitri and Vaska.

Vaska shrugged. "We figured now that you are a father to a girl, you've given up on life as you knew it."

"And you," I pointed to Dimitri, "take naps now in the middle of the afternoon. Ivan told me."

Dimitri cast Ivan a dirty look. Ivan just shrugged and took a large bite of his Egg McMuffin. "He asked how my meeting with you went."

Dimitri flashed a rude gesture before taking a sip of his coffee. "Emma is nine months pregnant. She gets tired." We continued to look at him. "We're at least naked," he burst out defensively.

They were all standing around a crate, on top of which they had placed their Egg McMuffins and hash browns like some kind of prison *obschhak* offering. At this point, it moved as a muffled sound came from it.

Dimitri kicked the crate. It went silent and still. He then pointed to me. "At least my woman wants to be with me. Your woman is so eager to get away from you, she jumped from a moving car yesterday."

I rubbed the back of my neck. "How the hell did you hear about that?"

Gregor looked up from wiping the baby vomit off his suit. "Rose is a terrible gossip. I thought you knew that."

Dimitri chimed in, "Gregor told me, and I told Vaska."

Vaska rocked back on his heels as he smiled. "And I told *everyone*."

"Rose isn't the only gossip around here," I grumbled.

The crate started up again.

This time Vaska pounded on the top and threatened, *"Ostanovis', ili ya otrezhu tvoy yazyk i skormlyu yego tebe."*

Again, the crate went silent and still.

Ivan rolled up his breakfast sandwich wrapper into a tiny ball as he spoke. "We finally got a lead on those PPK-20s from Kalashnikov that you wanted. I warn you, they are not as accurate as the Vityaz-Ms, but they only take 9x19mm ammo, so they are good for close combat."

Gregor nodded. "That is what my buyer wants. He needs something compact and small, but that can still fire over five hundred rounds a minute."

Ivan tossed the wrapper aside. "Then he shall have them. Delivery in three weeks."

Gregor slapped him on the back. "Good, my friend. We'll make a nice profit from those, especially if you can get the silencers."

"Done," said Ivan. "Our meeting for tonight is all set. The buyer is a pain in the ass, but he will be here with the cash."

Vaska grabbed a hash brown off the crate as he gave it another kick to stop the moaning. "Perhaps we can meet early and play some cards? It is not often we are all together."

"Not *Durak*," objected Dimitri as he gestured toward me. "You cleaned me out last time."

Vaska agreed. "Yes, you took my favorite watch from me that game."

I slid my suit jacket sleeve up. "It looks better on me, anyway. Fine, we'll play American poker." I inwardly smiled. They didn't know I was equally good at poker.

Gregor shook his head. "I have to get back to D.C. I don't like to leave Samara and the baby alone for too long."

The remark sobered us all. It was well known how fiercely protective Gregor was of both his wife and now his baby girl. Only something extremely serious would have brought him to Chicago in person on such short notice. He certainly wasn't here to oversee a simple gun buy.

Ivan's lips thinned. "Yes, enough socializing. Now we talk about the real reason you are here, and why you have brought this gift." He gestured to the crate, which moved again.

Gregor sighed. "We have a problem. Those cheap Chinese guns have shown up on the East Coast market as well. It is not an enterprising new gang, easily subdued as we had hoped. It is the yakuza."

I rubbed my neck. "Fuck."

The yakuza were a powerful Japanese crime syndicate. They usually stuck to drugs, human trafficking, and protection rackets. They knew guns were our territory.

Dimitri scowled. "Do we know which faction? It can't be the Yamaguchi-gumi. This is too small-time for them."

Gregor kicked the crate. "That is where our friend comes into play. Caught him right before he jumped on a private plane to Tokyo. His tattoos brand him as Inagawa-kai."

I nodded. "Makes sense. They are the smallest faction of the yakuza and have made the largest effort to expand outside of Japan to increase their influence. But why cheap Chinese guns? And why risk fucking with us?"

Gregor continued. "Apparently it was just opportunity. They got their hands on a container of the damn things and thought it would be a way to off-balance the market."

Vaska grimaced. "So they flood our market with crap, cause a bunch of issues, push the blame on us, and swoop in and steal our buyers with a supposedly superior product?"

Gregor nodded. "It looks like that was the plan. There's one more thing." He reached into his pocket and pulled out a wrinkled photo. He handed it to me. "We found a photo of you in his pocket. There's some writing on the back."

I flipped the photo over. In pencil were a few Japanese characters.

"It translates into a name, Kiyoshi Tanaka," said Gregor. "We think he might be the one assigned to target you. My intel tells me he's already here in Chicago."

Ivan let out a frustrated sigh. "It makes sense. You were the one looking into the matter for us."

Apparently, I had ruffled some feathers doing so. At least we knew I was on the right track.

My stomach twisted. For the first time in my life, I was worried. Not for me, but for Carinna. I lived a dangerous life and up until now, I'd only put myself at risk. My parents had no clue what I did for a living and were safely tucked away in a secure house I had purchased for them in a suburb of Moscow, far removed from my activities. Even the women in my life until this point had just been faceless bodies to keep my bed warm. Carinna was different. If my movements were being watched, then they would know about her.

Vaska's eyebrows rose. "Look on the bright side. They obviously are not very good at this. Who keeps a photo of the target? It's amateur hour."

I couldn't take that chance.

After the gun buy tonight, I would arrange to leave for Russia and take Carinna with me.

I doubted she would go willingly, which was why I had no plans to ask for her opinion. I would get her on the plane and convince her afterward. I would have her stay with my parents and double the covert security I had on the property. My parents were going to love her. I had never brought a woman home before, not even as a youth. They would immediately know what it meant, even if Carinna did not. I would not allow Carinna to be put in danger because of my work, but I also would not give her up, either. I could protect her, keep her safe. She would want for nothing.

Actually, the more I thought about it, the more I liked the idea. It would be far easier to keep her under control in my country than here. I could even arrange for someone to teach her about Russian pastries as I taught her the language. There was no reason why she couldn't have a cute little bakery in Moscow as she had intended to have one in Chicago. At least in Moscow, I could guarantee her success. I would make sure all of her suppliers provided her with free goods and would ensure she had an endless stream of willing and generous customers. Yes, the idea certainly had merit.

I tossed the photo onto the top of the crate. "If this asshole is here, we need to find him, and fast."

Dimitri pulled out his phone. "On it." He turned and walked a few steps away to have a conversation with his men.

Vaska turned to Gregor. "If we hit them, it has to be hard and decisive, but under the radar. I don't want this triggering bullshit violence in the streets. We need Mikhail."

Mikhail was the most experienced sniper in our crew. No one lived for long once Mikhail was on his trail.

Gregor shook his head. "Mikhail is in Venezuela, with Nadia handling that other issue for the U.S. government."

The primary reason why Gregor was based out of Washington, D.C. wasn't just because that was where the cesspool of humanity congregated to make back-room gun deals but also where governments from around the world, as well as the United States, could covertly reach out to us to handle certain delicate matters they would prefer not to involve their own military or spy agencies in. We often obliged since, in return, they would then turn a blind eye to our more profitable activities within their borders.

We were silent for a moment. Then Gregor said, "It has to be Luka."

Dimitri had returned by then and caught Gregor's last statement. "Fuck. You can't be serious."

"Who else then? We all know Luka will put an end to this quickly."

Vaska slowly shook his head. "Yes, but at what cost?"

I frowned. "Isn't he still locked up in some godforsaken Siberian prison?"

Gregor responded, "No. He got bored and left. He's in the States somewhere on a private contract, although I don't know where or what, but he'll come if I call."

"There's got to be another option," said Dimitri.

Gregor put his hand on Dimitri's shoulder. "I mean no disrespect, my friend. I know this is your city, your territory, but do you know how to track down a random Japanese man among millions of people? Because I sure as fuck don't. Luka has way more experience dealing with the yakuza than we do. It's only by luck we captured this asshole." Gregor kicked the crate.

This time, there was no moaning.

Vaska threw his hand up into the air. "He's right. With the new information about the yakuza being involved, this has gone from a minor nuisance to a possible all-out war. We no longer have the luxury of time. We need this handled. Quickly and decisively."

Dimitri rubbed his jaw. "Yes, I agree, but Luka... Once that beast is out of the cage, there is no putting him back in."

Vaska smirked. "Maybe his time in Siberia mellowed him."

We all laughed.

Ivan looked at his phone and frowned. "I have to go. It seems Dylan's family is making another move against her. Time to handle them once and for all."

I smiled. "Perhaps we can arrange for them to be tonight's entertainment?"

Ivan pointed at me. "I like how you think, my friend. Until tonight."

We all pivoted to return to our cars.

One of our men would see that they disposed of the crate where no one would ever find it.

As he opened the driver's side door, Vaska called out, "I'll bring the vodka."

We all groaned.

After making the arrangements for Luka's arrival, I headed for Carinna's pastry school.

I needed to see her.

The idea that I was being targeted and Carinna could get caught in the crosshairs rattled me more than I cared to admit.

CHAPTER 23

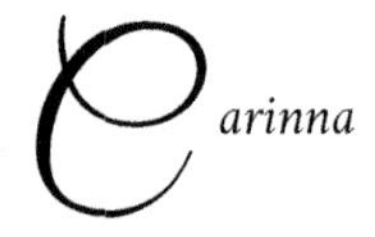

arinna

"WELL, HELLO AGAIN," tittered Chef Paulina.

The last time I heard her use that high-pitched voice… I looked up, then dropped my forehead onto a sack of flour.

Not again.

Avery elbowed me in the ribs. "Carinna, your super scary boyfriend is here again."

"He's not my boyfriend," I grumbled.

I didn't know what Maxim was, but boyfriend definitely didn't fit. Boyfriends took you to the movies and dinner dates to Olive Garden. They bought grocery store flowers and allowed themselves to be dragged to family barbecues. Boyfriends had boring jobs and liked to binge-watch shows on Netflix and annoy you by playing video games all night.

Boyfriends didn't wear two thousand-dollar suits and drag people to warehouses to be killed. They didn't wrap you up in duct tape and kidnap you. They didn't have pierced dicks and crazy ink and they definitely didn't throw you onto the bed and fuck your ass till you screamed for mercy.

Avery looked at me with a wide, unblinking stare.

I slapped my palm over my mouth. "Oh, my God, did I just say all that out loud?"

She slowly nodded. "I'm just going to go check on my rye bread starter."

She made a wide berth around Maxim as he approached, before practically running out of the room.

I lifted my white marble rolling pin and held it in front of me. "Don't you dare! I'm not leaving class again."

Maxim raised his hands up to his shoulders. "I'm just here to watch."

"Watch? Watch what?"

"You."

Dropping the rolling pin, I crossed my arms over my chest. "Well, you can't. There's no way my teacher will allow some random man to stand around and watch our class. Especially one who caused a disruption yesterday."

Maxim winked. "We'll just see about that."

He strolled back up to the front of the classroom.

I groaned as I watched my teacher pat the bun in her hair and bat her eyelashes at Maxim.

Maxim returned to my side just as Chef Paulina addressed the class. "Class, I'm delighted to say that we have a special guest today. Mr. Miloslavsky will be joining us and helping me..." she gripped her collar and breathed the next word, "*taste* all your endeavors."

I rolled my eyes. "Are you pleased with yourself? You've seduced an older *married* woman."

Maxim winked at me as his gaze became dark and hooded. "I'm always pleased with myself."

The double entendre made my stomach flip.

Chef Paulina spared me from having to answer. "Water,

yeast, flour, and salt and then you have bread. For this exercise, you will be hand kneading the bread. Only use the mixer to mix the ingredients. We get back to basics. In order to *know* bread, you must first *feel* the bread. Now, begin!"

I had gotten to class early and already prepared my ingredients. I needed to make up for yesterday's embarrassing display. Doing my best to ignore the giant mass of tattooed muscle at my elbow, I turned my assigned oven on to two hundred degrees and added my flour and salt to the mixer.

Maxim leaned over my shoulder and whispered into my ear, "Do you know you bite your lower lip when you're trying to concentrate?"

I shrugged my shoulder in an effort to put him off as I added my warm water to a clean glass bowl.

He switched to the other shoulder. "You also bite your lip just before you come."

"Stop it," I hissed.

Chef Paulina looked up. "Is there a problem, Miss Russo?"

"No, Chef."

I picked up my small glass bowl and scraped the three tablespoons of honey into the water and then added a cup of warm whole milk.

Maxim ran his fingers down the center of my back, just grazing the top of my ass. "I can think of at least a dozen more pleasurable ways to use that honey."

"You promised to behave," I whispered over my shoulder as I reached for the yeast and butter to add to my warm liquid mixture.

Maxim tugged on a curl that had fallen out of my bun. "I promised no such thing."

Trying my best to concentrate, I mixed the butter and yeast in before very slowly pouring it into the flour while the mixer was on low.

Maxim leaned in. His hard cock brushed my hip.

"What are you doing?" I asked through clenched teeth.

He placed his large hand on my lower back. "Just trying to get a better view."

He shifted his hips, firmly pressing his shaft against my body.

My eyelids briefly fluttered closed as I remembered how his hard cock felt ramming into me just on the other side of that wall, while I was sprawled out on the dean's desk like a freaking wanton.

I swallowed as I willed myself to concentrate.

Chef Paulina called out to the class, "Don't overmix your flour mixture."

Maxim's voice was a low, seductive growl. "Did you hear that, babygirl? Don't overmix, or I might just have to give you a spanking." His hand gently patted my right ass cheek.

"Oh, God," I called out a little too loudly.

Chef Paulina headed in my direction. "What seems to be the problem, Miss Russo?" Although the question was directed at me, her entire focus was on Maxim.

"Nothing, Chef. I thought I had overmixed."

Maxim interjected. "It was probably my fault. I find learning about all this baking very *stimulating*." He squeezed my ass with his right hand. The position of our bodies hid his movements.

I inhaled sharply as my cheeks burned.

She surveyed my flour mixture. "No. It is perfect. Remove from the bowl and knead. And remember, knead too little and your bread will not rise and be too dense. Knead too much, you kill the flavor."

"Yes, Chef." I hurried to follow her instructions, deliberately shifting away, breaking Maxim's grip on my ass.

I spread a light dusting of flour on the stainless steel countertop. Lifting the top of the mixer, I grabbed the bowl and used a spatula to scrape the contents onto my flour.

Rolling up my chef coat sleeves, I kneaded the sticky mixture.

Maxim stepped behind me. His hands cupped my shoulders as his cock pressed into my lower back. Unfortunately, the motion of kneading rocked my body back and forth slowly.

I heard his sharp intake of breath.

My lips twisted into a smirk. I guess two could play at this game.

I leaned over the counter, pushing my ass out as I put more pressure on the flour mixture.

Maxim's hand shifted to grip my hip. "Careful, babygirl," he warned.

I did it again. Then a third time. This time I added a low throaty moan for his ears only.

Maxim leaned over me. "If you think I won't bend you over this counter and fuck you raw while I spank your impertinent ass in front of this entire fucking class, then you haven't been paying attention," he growled.

I turned to face him, my hands covered in sticky dough. I opened my eyes wide as I batted my eyelashes. "Why, Mr. Miloslavsky, I don't know what you mean. I'm just *kneading my bread.*"

His eyes narrowed as he tilted his head to the right. His fiery gaze traveled from my eyes down to my toes and back. "I'll *knead your bread.*"

My breath caught in my throat. I was definitely playing a dangerous game. I didn't doubt for a moment he would make good on his threat and fuck me right here and now, in front of all my classmates. Once they got a look at his pierced cock and rock-hard abs, they'd probably cheer him on.

I swiftly pivoted and returned to actually kneading my bread.

Chef Paulina's voice sounded a world away. "Do not give into the temptation..."

My mouth dropped open.

Holy shit... is she talking about us?

Did she see what we are doing?

Oh, my God, is she....

Chef Paulina then finished her instructions. "...to add too much flour while you are kneading. The dough may be sticky at first, but once the water evenly distributes as you knead, the flour will absorb it and the dough will become soft and silky to the touch."

Maxim ran his finger over my exposed wrist and forearm. "Soft and silky, two of my favorite words."

Heat pooled between my legs. What the fuck? What was this? A historical romance? Where my heart pitter-patters over the touch of his hand on mine, or a scandalous flash of ankle?

Feeling overheated, I brushed my cheek with the back of my wrist as I continued to knead. This time I kept my hips and back rigidly straight.

Maxim placed his hands over mine. I looked up.

He rubbed his thumb across my cheekbone. "You have flour on your cheek."

His gaze moved from my cheek to my lips.

My mouth opened as I swept my tongue over my dry lips.

A low rumbling growl emanated from deep inside his chest. "Just wait till I get you home, *moya malen'kaya iskra*."

I squeezed my inner thighs tight as a rush of arousal made my head swim.

He placed his hands on my shoulders and pushed me back slightly. For one minute, I thought he meant to push me back onto the countertop and fuck me senseless, and in that crazy minute I would have let him do it and damn the consequences.

Maxim shrugged out of his suit jacket and tossed it aside. He rolled up the sleeves of his dress shirt, exposing his heavily tattooed and muscled forearms. I could see the faint outline of where I bit him right before he fucked my ass and shattered my world.

Stepping up to the counter, he pushed the heels of his palms into the dough mixture and slowly and methodically kneaded.

My throat went dry as a hot flush crept over my chest and up my cheeks.

He worked the dough with his firm hands. Squeezing and massaging it. Caressing it back into the bowl before flattening it with his palms. Repeatedly. At one point, he picked it up, twisted it, and slapped it against the counter.

I cried out as my hand went to my chest.

The sound the dough made smacking against the metal counter wasn't that far off from the sound of skin hitting skin when he spanked me with his bare hand.

Flushed, my gaze skittered around the kitchen to see if anyone observed us. Every student in the class had stopped what they were doing and stood, mesmerized, by the unmistakably sexual motion of Maxim's hands as he kneaded my dough.

After several minutes, he stopped. He reached for a nearby kitchen towel and wiped his hands.

Chef Paulina cleared her throat, breaking the tension in the room. She clapped her hands. "Class, get back to your dough."

Maxim stepped up to me. My ass pressed against the counter edge as he placed a hand on either side of my hips.

I licked my lips again. "Where did you… where did you learn to knead dough like that?"

He kept his gaze on my mouth. "Despite what you may

think, I wasn't a motherless mongrel. All good Russian children learn to bake bread from their mama or babushka."

I didn't hear a word he said.

All I kept thinking was *kiss me, kiss me, kiss me.*

"I have to get back to..." I couldn't form the words.

Maxim stepped aside, leaving me feeling strangely cold and bereft.

I placed the dough into an oiled bowl and covered it before putting it in the oven to rise.

While the class waited for our doughs to rise and then later, while they were in the oven baking, Maxim entertained everyone with funny stories about his friends. I wondered if everyone would laugh so lightheartedly at their antics if they knew these same men were the ones who'd just killed a man in cold blood? Not that I lamented the death of Dylan's uncle or had thought for one moment to go to the police about it. The police would only involve Dylan and cause problems. As far as I was concerned, what was done was done, and there was no point in getting the authorities involved. Still, that didn't mean I was okay with being with a man who was capable of such violence.

When the breads were finished, all the female students crowded around Maxim, offering him a slice and asking his opinion. Maxim obliged by tasting each and every one and complimenting the women.

"Which one did you like the best?" asked one student.

Keeping his gaze trained on me, he reached for my loaf of bread. He tore off a sizeable chunk and sank his teeth into the soft, warm, white crust. "I could eat this one, and nothing else, for the rest of my life."

I dug my nails into the palms of my hands.

Only the sharp sting of pain kept me from fainting dead away.

* * *

THE REST of class was a blur. I didn't even remember the drive home. All I remembered was Maxim, slamming me against the wall in my apartment's hallway and kissing me senseless while he groped in his pocket for the key to the door. His piercing clattered against my front teeth as our tongues fought for dominance.

My head rocked back as he kissed my neck. "Fuck it. Just kick the damn thing down."

"Don't tempt me."

He finally got the door unlocked.

We tumbled inside, each grabbing for the other's clothes. Maxim kicked off his shoes as he ripped at the buttons on my chef's coat. The ping of plastic rattling across my scarred hardwood floors was the only sound heard over our heavy breathing as I tore open his shirt, sending the buttons flying.

I kissed his chest, loving the tang on my tongue from his metal nipple piercings.

Maxim picked me up. My legs wrapped around his hips as he carried me to the bedroom. I sucked on his neck like a teenager, not caring if I left a hickey.

He dropped me onto the center of the bed. I bounced up onto my knees and grabbed for his belt buckle. His hands stilled mine. "Slow down, *moya lyubimaya*. This time, I want to savor your charms."

Paralyzing fear crept over my limbs as alarm bells went off in my head.

No. No. No.

I couldn't allow him to make love to me.

That would be a disaster.

Right now, the only thing keeping me from falling completely head over heels in love with this man was the guilt and confusion over the filthy, raw sex we usually had. It was easy to put him in a tiny box labeled *bad boy mistakes* when he was slapping my ass and calling me his dirty little whore. I couldn't have him gently making love to me and calling me his beloved in Russian. That would make him a boyfriend… or something even more serious.

In desperation, I tore at his belt buckle and lowered the zipper of his pants. I reached inside and pulled his long shaft free. Raising my gaze to clash with his, I opened my mouth wide and deliberately clattered the edge of my teeth over his piercing before licking the head of his cock.

"Are you sure you don't want to force this big… hard… cock down my tiny throat?" I breathed.

"God dammit," he snarled as he reached for my hair. He twisted it painfully before demanding, "Open your mouth, dirty girl."

CHAPTER 24

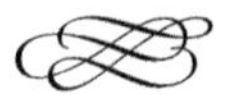

Maxim

I WOKE UP ANGRY.

Sex with Carinna last night had been amazing, as it always was. Never had I ever fucked a woman so hard or so completely. She was quite simply the best fucking sex I'd ever had. Yet, for the first time in my life, I wanted something more. Something beyond just the hair pulling and hard thrusts. I couldn't believe I was even thinking this girly shit, but I wanted a *connection* with her. I craved a deeper bond.

And she'd blown me off. Literally.

She'd grabbed my dick and distracted me with that hot little mouth of hers.

And now I was pissed.

She was trying to keep me at arm's length. Lord knew I had given her plenty of fucking reasons to do so, but that didn't matter to me. There was something between us, something deeper, and I would not let her push me away or shut me out.

As I pushed the covers aside, I heard her voice in the kitchen. It was clear she was agitated and trying to whisper.

"I'll get you the money," she said urgently.

What the fuck?

"I just need more time. I… I… lost my job this week."

Yeah, because of me. If my babygirl needed money, she knew I was more than ready to give her however much she wanted. I reached for the pair of jeans I had in my duffle bag.

Carinna continued her whispered conversation. "I know. I know. You don't have to say such mean things. I give you as much money as I can. It's just hard right now with tuition and rent."

I pulled my jeans on, not bothering to zip them up. When I entered the kitchen, her back was turned to me.

She cried out, "I'm not being selfish. I told you I'd get you the money."

I walked up behind her and ripped the phone from her grasp. "Who the fuck is this?" I growled.

An older woman's voice came over the line. "Who the hell is this?"

I pulled the phone from my ear and looked at the screen. Maria Russo.

Before I could respond, Maria ordered, "Put my ungrateful daughter back on the phone."

Carinna tried to reach for the phone. I held it out of her reach. "Who is this bitch, Carinna?"

Carinna stretched her arm again, reaching for the phone. "Oh, my God! She's my mother! Don't say that so loud. She'll hear you!"

We could both hear her mother scream through the phone.

Ignoring it, I focused my attention on Carinna. "Why is she demanding money from you?"

Carinna's eyes filled with tears. "Please, just give me the phone. I'm handling it."

My fingers squeezed the phone so hard I'm surprised the screen didn't crack.

She was crying. My babygirl was crying.

I put the phone back to my ear. "Why are you asking your daughter for money?"

"That selfish bitch knows why. She owes us!"

Closing my eyes, I desperately tried to keep a rein on my temper. I turned to Carinna. "What is she talking about?"

Carinna crossed her arms over her chest and looked away. "Nothing. It's a family matter."

"Is this for your tuition?"

Fuck, I had planned on handling that for her. It was the least I could do after turning her life upside down and costing her her job these last few days. I'd gotten distracted with Dylan's uncle and the threat of the yakuza in our territory. Later today, I would swing by her school and pay the rest of her tuition for the year and any semesters she had left until her degree. I would then pay her horrible parents back for whatever money she may have borrowed from them.

Carinna's chin jutted up. "No. I pay my tuition. They've never given me a cent."

"Then, what? Tell me now, Carinna." I was losing patience, and that didn't bode well for my temper.

A voice crackled over the phone. "Is this your new boyfriend? What's the matter, Carinna? Don't want to tell him you're a selfish, lying *murderer*? Don't want to tell him how you killed Carlo? How you took him away from us?"

Carinna squeezed her eyes shut as a tear escaped and trickled down her cheek. She turned her back on me as she swiped at her cheeks.

I tossed the phone aside and snatched Carinna to my chest. Cradling her head next to my heart, I swallowed to clear my throat. My voice was hoarse when I demanded, "Tell me."

Her voice warbled as she sighed, then responded. "I'm the reason my brother Carlo is dead. There was an accident. A car accident. I pay my parents money because they say I owe them. If I hadn't killed my brother, he'd be helping support them."

Her mother continued to shout and scream obscenities over the phone.

Keeping my arms tightly around Carinna, I reached to pick up the phone. "Listen to me very carefully, Maria."

Carinna shook her head violently. "No! Please don't!"

I turned her head against my chest, muffling her.

"If you don't repay every cent your daughter has given you, I will track you down and take away what little you have left in your pathetic life. Do you understand me?"

Maria uttered a shocked gasp. "Who the hell are you?"

I tightened my grip on Carinna. "I'm the man who is going to marry your daughter and if you don't repay her money and adjust your attitude, I will see to it you never lay eyes on her or our children. Ever. Have I made myself clear?"

Carinna stared up at me with wide eyes.

Maria fired back, "Carinna would never allow that."

"I am the one who will make the rules in our house," I growled back. "And I can assure you, you could lay on your deathbed, begging for her, and I still wouldn't allow you to see her, unless you make this right."

"How dare you speak to me this way!"

This time, I raised my voice. I was out of patience. "How dare you treat your daughter this way! Pay her back her money or lose this fucking number."

I then hung up the call and tossed the phone onto the

counter as if it were poison. I added getting Carinna a new phone and phone number to my list of things to accomplish today. I didn't even like the idea of her holding that phone ever again.

Carinna backed away from me as she clutched her chest and hyperventilated. "What… what just happened?"

I took a tentative step toward her, arms raised. "Carinna."

She held up a hand as she backed away. "Don't Carinna me. What did you just do?"

"I told your toxic mother where she could stick it."

"She already hates me. Now she's going to hate me even more. Giving them money was the only thing that kept them in my life."

"Good. You don't need them in your life. You have me."

I took several more steps toward her. Hating seeing her like this, I reached for her.

Carinna balled up her fists and slammed them against my chest. "No! Don't!"

I snatched her close. "Shhh… baby. I've got you."

She clutched at me and cried. I picked her up and carried her over to the sofa. I sat and cradled her in my arms, letting her cry it out as I stroked her hair and whispered words of love in Russian that she would not understand.

She kept her head lowered when she spoke. "The car accident was my fault."

I tried to object, but she stopped me.

"It was. I was sixteen and stupid. I had snuck out to see some boy. He made a pass, and I got scared. I ran off and called my brother to come pick me up. We got into an accident on his way back from picking me up. My parents have never forgiven me. Carlo was their golden boy."

I cupped her jaw and lifted her face. "Baby, that wasn't your fault."

She objected. "It was! It was! He never would have been in his car at that intersection if it hadn't been for me."

"And what if you hadn't called him for help?"

"What do you mean?"

"What if you hadn't called? What if you had stayed in that dangerous situation and that piece of shit boy had beat you or raped you or worse? What do you think that would have done to your brother?"

She started. "No one has ever asked me that. It would have destroyed Carlo. I was his baby sister. He was very protective of me."

I smoothed her hair back and stroked her tearstained cheeks. "Then don't take that away from him."

Her lower lip trembled, but I could see I was getting through to her.

I continued, "Your brother was being a big brother. He was looking after you. Protecting you. I am sure if he had it to do all over again, he'd make the same decision, knowing that no matter what happened, in the end, at least you were safe. Baby, don't take that act of heroism from his memory. Don't let your parents take that from him, either."

She sniffed as she burrowed her head into the crook of my neck. "Thank you," she whispered.

I caressed her back. "Is this why you refuse anyone's help? Why you think you should do all this on your own?"

She shrugged. "The last time I asked for help, it killed my brother. Besides, it's more than that."

"What else is there?"

She shrugged again as she ran her fingertip through the dark hair in the center of my chest. "I don't know. That I'm supposed to be an independent woman. That I'm not supposed to need or rely on a man. That I'm supposed to make it on my own two feet."

"Bullshit."

She huffed. "You can't say that."

"Bullshit."

"Stop saying that. You can't say bullshit to a hundred years of women's suffrage and feminism."

I smirked. "Try me. Your idea of feminism is not the Russian way."

"And what is the *Russian* way?"

"The Russian way is to take care of a woman. She should not have to work. Her man should take care of all of her needs. Her only job is to please him and to raise his children."

"That's absurd and sexist and misogynistic."

I pushed her hair off her shoulder as I stroked the back of my knuckles down her soft neck. "It's what I believe."

I wasn't saying a woman couldn't have a job or a business. It was just that any woman I called my own wouldn't have to have them. She would know that I was taking care of her. Anything she chose to do would be for her own pleasure and not for her own survival. And of course, no job or business would be allowed to come between her and my needs. After all, what was the point of having millions of dollars if you couldn't spend it on those you love and want to protect?

She laughed as she got up off my lap. She swiped her palm over her cheeks. "Then I guess it's a good thing you were just messing with my mother when you told her you were going to marry me."

I stood and towered over her. I wrapped an arm around her waist and pulled her close. Placing a finger under her chin, I raised her face to mine. "Who said I was kidding?"

CHAPTER 25

arinna

"AND THEN HE said he wasn't kidding!"

"Shut up!"

"I know, right? How fucking crazy is that?"

I was sitting in the back of my favorite café down the street from my apartment, on the phone with Dylan. I would have liked to have met up with her in person, but Ivan wasn't letting her leave the hotel after some big incident involving him and a poker game.

"Do you think he's serious?"

I picked at my croissant. "No. Of course not. I've known the man for less than a week. He's just trying to rattle my cage."

Dylan remained silent.

"*You* don't actually think he's serious, do you?" I asked.

She sighed into the phone. "All I know is that these Russian men are nothing like the American men we've dated.

They don't seem to have the same hang-ups with serious relationships and marriage. I wouldn't put it past Maxim to actually be serious about marrying you."

My eyes narrowed. "Why are you saying this? Has Ivan proposed to you?"

She snorted. "No, of course not."

I put a hand to my chest. "That's a relief."

"But he has implied it."

I pulled off a large buttery piece of croissant and popped it into my mouth. "Would you marry him if he asked you?"

"Would you think I was crazy if I said yes?"

"Yes."

"Then, yes."

"You would actually marry a man you only just met?"

"No one's saying we'd have to marry right away, but why not? Ivan is amazing. He's fucking intense as hell, but he's also really protective and funny and sweet and charming."

She could be describing my feelings about Maxim. Not willing to face those yet, I brushed her off. "This is stupid. Are we actually talking about a couple of uber-hot kajillionaire Russian men getting so swept off their feet by the two of us that they propose their undying love and say they want to marry us?"

Dylan laughed. "You're right. Can you see the two of us splitting our time between our mansions in Moscow and here in Chicago?"

Warming up to the joke, I added, "Or meeting for lunch as we compare the latest piece of Cartier jewelry they bought us."

"Daahhhhrrrlllinng, you simply must join us on the yacht this summer," teased Dylan.

I took a sip of my cappuccino. "Meanwhile, back in the real world, I need to find myself a jobby-job. Maybe now that I'm a few semesters into the pastry degree program, I should try applying again as a pastry chef at some restaurant?"

"You totally should. You're amazing. Once they taste your strawberry Fraisier cake, they will fall over themselves trying to hire you. In the meantime, and don't get upset or offended, but do you need a loan to get by?"

"Why? Did you listen to me and hold back some of that money your uncle sent you before Ivan snatched it back?"

"No, but I have a little money saved in my Ann Taylor LOFT fund. I know your parents are going to make you miserable if you don't send them something this month."

"Yeah, about that. Maxim sort of told off my mom this morning."

"Shut up! Tell me everything. I've been wanting to tell that bitch to go to hell for years."

I played with the edge of my paper napkin. "Later. That is a conversation for tequila shots, not lukewarm cappuccino."

"Speaking of which, how are you at a café right now? Ivan told me," and now she mimicked a deep Russian accent, "all our women are on lockdown. It's why I'm stuck in this stupid hotel."

"Yeah, Maxim said," and I also did a Russian accent, "do not leave this apartment or there'll be hell to pay when I return."

Dylan sighed into the phone. "They're so dramatic."

"Right?"

"So you just left? Lucky. I have a freaking guard outside my door right now."

I looked to the left through the café's store window. Standing outside was a large man smoking a cigarette, glaring at anyone who passed. "I have a guard, too. I just waltzed past him and strolled to the café. Poor guy. I don't think he knew what to do!"

"You're so bad! Maxim is going to be pissed."

"Let him be pissed," I responded with more bravado than I felt.

A vision of him stripping off his belt and telling me to bend over for my punishment flashed before my mind. I squeezed my legs together. Truth be told I had gotten bored and more than a little peevish about being told to stay put like a child. So I'd grabbed my backpack and purse and boldly left the apartment. The moment I got on the street, I regretted my rash act but couldn't back down. The stupid bodyguard was already on the phone with Maxim. I didn't understand Russian, but I knew when I was being ratted out. Since the damage was done, I figured I might as well have a last meal at my favorite café.

Wanting to change the subject, I said, "Did I tell you Maxim showed up at my class?"

"Oh, my God, what did sourpuss Chef Paulina do?"

I scoffed, "Besides shamelessly flirt with him, nothing. Anyway, we were making bread and holy shit it was like the scene from the movie *Ghost* but with bread dough instead of clay. He—"

At that moment, I was interrupted. A tall, slender Japanese man in a very expensive-looking suit came up to my table.

"Hold on one sec, Dylan. Can I help you?"

He had a long, pale face and deep brown, almost black hooded eyes. "Please pardon my intrusion. I couldn't help but overhear your conversation. I understand you are looking for a position as a pastry chef. This is extremely fortuitous. I own a restaurant and am in desperate need of one."

What luck!

"Dylan, I have to call you back."

Without waiting for her to respond, I hung up the phone. I gestured for the man to have a seat as I moved my schoolbooks out of the way.

He gestured toward the top book. "*Our Lady of Perpetual Hunger* was an intriguing read."

"You've read Lisa Donovan's book? I'm a big fan of her work."

He smiled as he reached for the book to look at the cover. I noticed he had a brightly colored tattoo of a snake coiled around his wrist. When he saw the direction of my gaze, he pulled down his shirt cuff, hiding it.

"My restaurant is only just down the street. Perhaps we could go there and talk about the position and salary. It would also give you a chance to see the kitchen and menu."

I hesitated. It was getting dark outside, and Maxim would probably return soon. I then caught a glance of the guard pacing outside the café. Well, it wasn't like I wasn't being guarded. What harm could come from seeing his restaurant? It was a public space, after all, and besides, I needed a job.

"That sounds wonderful." I held out my hand. "I'm Carinna Russo, by the way."

He took my hand. His grasp was limp and cold. "Pleasure to meet you, Ms. Russo. My name is Kiyoshi Tanaka."

CHAPTER 26

axim

"Where the hell is he?" I asked as I stomped out a cigarette on the side of the road.

I was eager to get back to Carinna. This yakuza mess had me on edge. I had already made arrangements to fly her to Moscow tomorrow night. I hadn't decided whether I was going to tell her about my plans or just toss her over my shoulder and carry her onto the plane. I had a feeling option B was going to be the winner. There was no fucking way she would agree to leave school and her apartment with no notice, simply because I demanded it.

It was one thing I loved about her. She was so fucking stubborn. I hadn't realized how boring it was to always have a woman agree and obey you until I'd found one who'd rather set herself on fire than admit I was right about something. Damn, she was fun to be around.

Ivan took a long drag off of his. "He'll be here."

"Any reason why we had to meet him in the middle of nowhere and not inside a nice warm bar?"

Ivan shrugged. "You know Luka. He's not much for civilized society."

"That's an understatement."

Luka Siderov wasn't exactly the talkative socializing type, but there was no better man to have on your side when you needed a job done. Just as long as you didn't care how that job got done. He was not known for his subtlety. The phrase bull in a china shop was made for this guy. When you hired him, things got bloody and messy. No way around it. On the other hand, he was the best choice to send a clear message to the yakuza to back the fuck off our territory.

My phone rang. "Yes?"

The guard I had placed on Carinna's apartment spoke to me in rapid-fire Russian.

I rubbed my eyes. "Did you tell her to get back inside?"

"She wouldn't listen, boss."

"So you just let her stroll right by you and out of the building?"

"Yes, boss."

"And she's, what? Five foot six and maybe a hundred and thirty-five pounds?"

"Uh huh."

"And you're what?"

"Six foot two and just under three hundred," came the reluctant reply.

I let out a frustrated sigh. "Tell me, Boris. What was the point of paying you to guard her?"

"I'm sorry, boss. Do you want me to drag her back inside?"

"No. Don't fucking lay a finger on her."

That was my job. The moment I got home, I was going to tie her to the bed and spank her ass raw for this. My cock hardened and lengthened against my inner thigh at the thought. I made a mental note to pick up some lube on the way home. I was going to teach her a lesson about obedience she'd never forget. If she was going to be my girl, she needed to understand that there were times I needed her to obey me, no questions asked. I had a feeling that would be a lesson I would have to teach her over and over and over again. My palm itched just thinking about it.

Sighing again, I said, "Just follow her and keep a close eye on her. Make sure she doesn't get into any trouble and keep me posted."

"Yes, boss."

I hung up the phone.

Ivan smirked. "Trouble in paradise?"

"Fuck you. Like you have it so easy."

Ivan pulled out his phone and made a show of dialing a number. The moment someone answered, he asked, "Is Dylan safe inside the hotel room?"

"Yes, boss."

Ivan's eyebrow rose as he looked over at me.

I gave him my middle finger.

Ivan finished the call. "Good. See that it stays that way."

I tapped my finger against my lips. "What was it again that Dylan called out when she busted up our meeting the other night and caused a huge firefight that ended in Dimitri's wife going into labor? What was it she said?" I asked, pretending to think. "Oh, yeah, I remember. *Stop! Police!*"

Ivan smirked as he gave me his middle finger. "Fuck you."

"Are you coming back to Moscow with me tomorrow or staying here?"

Ivan nodded. "If I can convince Dylan to come with me."

I puffed out my chest. "You see, that's where we differ. I don't plan on asking Carinna's permission."

Ivan laughed as he tossed his cigarette aside. "Let me know how that turns out for you."

Just then a massive eighteen-wheeler truck rolled into view. It was the first sign of life we had seen on this road all night.

I nodded in the truck's direction. "Could that be him?"

As the truck passed, the back door rolled up. Two heavy loose chains dragged along the tarmac, sending bright sparks blazing on either side of the tires. Inside the dark cavernous space, a single headlight flicked on. There was a roar of an engine.

A massive black motorcycle leapt from the back of the still-moving truck. The moment it hit the road, the tires screeched and the back end fishtailed before righting itself. The motorcycle sprang forward, careening down the road for at least a quarter of a mile before whipping around and returning to where we stood.

The eighteen-wheeler continued down the road as if nothing had happened. Only the sound of the truck's horn showed the driver even knew the motorcycle was no longer on board.

Everything returned to a still darkness.

Luka stood, straddling his Indian Chief Dark Horse motorcycle. He reached into his coat pocket and pulled out a silver case. He selected a cigarette and placed it between his lips. He lit it before saying, "We have a problem."

I patted down my suit pockets. "Hold on. I'm looking for a pair of panties to throw at you after that entrance."

Luka flashed us a rare smile. He wrapped his hand around my neck and pressed his forehead to mine. "It is good to see you too, my friend."

Ivan interjected, "What's the latest?"

Luka climbed off his motorcycle and joined us to lean against our car. "You are familiar with the Novikoff?"

I nodded. "Of course. Egor, the head of the family, used to have an operation on the East Coast. Pain in the ass. He went home to Russia and left his idiot sons in charge. They made a fucking mess of things. Then there is his daughter Katie, but I know for a fact she's not in the life."

Ivan spoke. "Lenin and Leonid Novikoff are both dead. Mikhail took them out last year when they tried to kidnap Gregor's little sister."

Luka nodded again. "True. The problem is with the sister."

My brow furrowed. "Katie's involved with this?"

Luka corrected me. "Her name is Katia and yes." His lips thinned. "The yakuza kidnapped her over a week ago from her college dorm. Egor hired me to find her. I've tracked her here to Chicago."

I ran a hand through my hair. "Fuck. We didn't know."

I looked at Ivan, who just stood there, rubbing his fist inside his palm. "So this confirms they are playing dirty. They're going after the women to force our hand."

Luka continued. "They brought her here to Chicago because they have another target. They're planning on taking both women back to Japan to use as leverage against our organization."

Another target? That could be any of the girls here in Chicago: Emma, Mary, Carinna, or Dylan.

Ivan pulled out his phone to call Dylan.

I pulled out mine to call Carinna.

No answer.

I called her guard, Boris.

No answer.

CHAPTER 27

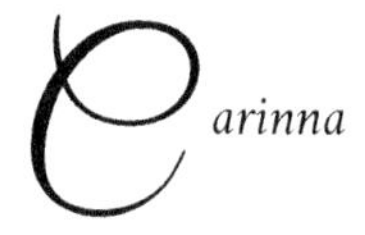

arinna

I WAS sure my mind was playing tricks on me. It was Maxim's fault. He had gotten into my head with all this *Goodfellas* mafia movie stuff. Somehow the usually noisy and bustling city seemed to have fallen silent. Where I typically had to shoulder my way down a sidewalk, there wasn't a soul in sight. Night had fallen. All the store windows were dark. The winter weather made it seem even more quiet and gloomy.

I played with the strap of my backpack. "So, what's the name of your restaurant?"

The man by my side didn't respond.

I glanced over my shoulder, relieved to see my guard shadowing me.

Never thought I'd say that.

I had been planning on giving Maxim a piece of my mind when he returned. I mean, the balls on that man putting a freaking armed guard on my apartment, especially without telling me. I only realized the guy was there when I opened the door to leave, defying Maxim's direct order. I mean, sure, Maxim had commanded me to stay inside until he returned, but it was a matter of pride. Up until that moment, I had planned on studying at home until Maxim had ordered me to do so. Then I had no choice but to put on a pair of jeans and head out to the café.

I didn't know who had been more shocked when I swung open the door: me or the guard.

By then I couldn't back down. I needed to prove to Maxim that he couldn't treat me like this. I wasn't some piece of property that needed guarding. I had gotten along just fine in life until him. I was an independent woman and was free to go and see and do whatever I damned well pleased. Well, that was what I had planned on telling him. Now I couldn't be more relieved that someone had my back.

Goosebumps pricked along my arms as an uneasy feeling settled in my stomach.

I carefully reached inside my purse, searching for the handle of the gun Maxim had given me.

Wait. Is this crazy?

Sure, this had probably been a mistake. I should have just gotten this guy's card and Googled his restaurant and then emailed him to set up an interview instead of just blindly following him out into the night. I had just been so desperate for a legitimate job it had overridden my good sense, which was now crashing back down on me.

But to pull a gun on the guy?

Maxim's comments about my bartending job being beneath me had really hit home. I wanted a career. I wanted my own bakery one day. I wanted to make something of my life, in a way that would have made my brother proud. I wanted to show I hadn't wasted the second chance I had gotten when I survived the accident and he didn't. Maxim yelling at my mother finally shook me out of my malaise. It made me realize the only reason why I was a bartender was because of my parents' demands for money. I took the job because I needed something that paid well with short hours to keep up with them and my rent and my tuition. But that job wasn't doing anything to further my career.

I should have done what Maxim did today and told them to fuck off long ago. I should have realized my big brother would have wanted me to follow my dreams, not cater to our parents' greed. Snatching at the opportunity that Kiyoshi Tanaka had dropped into my lap seemed like fate. A legitimate pastry chef job. A start to my career. Plus, I wouldn't feel like I had given in to Maxim. The last thing I wanted was to become a kept woman. If whatever this was between Maxim and me was going to work, he'd need to understand that I needed to earn my own money and make my own way.

Wow. That was the first time I had even thought about the possibility of a future with Maxim. I was so rigid in putting him in that one-night stand box. Even though he had repeatedly made it clear he was not a one-night stand. I didn't even know how a relationship between us would work.

I mean, he lived in Russia.

I lived in America.

He lived in this strange world of money, power, and crime.

I lived in the real world of bills, jobs, and laws.

That's right. The real world.

In the real world, people didn't pull guns on someone offering them a job simply because they got the heebie-jeebies on a dark winter's night.

I mean, sure, Mr. Tanaka was acting a little weird and awkward, but this was Chicago. The city was filled with weird and awkward people, especially in the hospitality industry. My industry was like a circus filled with freaks and geeks and criminals and all sorts of people.

Who did I think I was? Some gangster's moll like in a black and white movie? Like I'm suddenly Barbara Stanwyck ready to whip out my revolver and tell him to aim 'em high?

What would I have done before Maxim?

I would have just walked away. No gun needed.

That's what I would do. Just walk away.

I cleared my throat. "You know what? On second thought, it's getting pretty late. Maybe we can schedule a time tomorrow for me to see the place?"

I stopped and turned back toward the safety of the café.

Kiyoshi grabbed my upper arm.

"Hey, let go!" I turned to scream for help.

The guard who had been following us sprang into action. He reached into his coat pocket. There was a loud blast of sound. My ears rang as the smell of sulfur surrounded us.

The guard stopped, a look of stunned shock and confusion on his face.

Then a burst of red spread out from the center of his chest, like some macabre rose. He pitched forward and fell face-first onto the pavement.

In horror, I looked at Kiyoshi. He was standing at my side, a gun drawn at his hip. He raised the gun higher and stuck it into my ribs just as a black sedan pulled up to the curb. "Get in the fucking car."

I knew if I got in that car, I was as good as dead. I swung to the right as I raised my knee, catching him in the groin. As he bent over, I made a run for it. Dropping my backpack and purse, I raced back toward the café, the only lit storefront down the mostly abandoned side street.

A hard weight hit me from behind. My knees slammed into the cold pavement first. I raised my arms to block my fall, scraping my palms. A hand wrapped around my ankle, pulling me backward. I flipped onto my back and kicked out, catching him under the jaw. Kiyoshi's head snapped back.

I scrambled to my feet and ran. I only got a few steps before something slammed me against the building to my left. I screamed in pain as my left arm hung limp. I slumped to the ground. My entire arm and hand went numb. I looked down to see my shoulder distended. The pain was so intense, I thought I might vomit.

A second Japanese man I didn't recognize stood over me. He had the same pale complexion and a similar expensive suit as Kiyoshi, but his build was much larger. Unlike Kiyoshi's refined slim features, his nose was broad and flat. He was also missing several teeth in the front.

The man reached down and gripped me by my injured arm, lifting me to my feet.

I screamed in pain as bile rose in the back of my throat. Darkness shaded the edges of my vision. I fought to maintain consciousness. I couldn't faint right now. I couldn't. I needed to stay alert, no matter how much the sweet darkness called to me. In darkness, there would be no pain, no fear. I could hide in the darkness. No. I fought the urge to give in.

The man said something in Japanese.

Not understanding the words but inferring the meaning, I gathered a glob of saliva on my tongue and spit it at his face. "Fuck you."

The man yanked on my arm.

My knees buckled as I fell to the sidewalk.

The man then kicked me in the stomach.

This time I vomited. My only consolation was I did so on the asshole's shiny black shoes.

As I lay curled up on the cold cement, I watched as he shifted his foot backward. He was going to kick me again, but I couldn't summon up the energy to move out of the way or protect myself. The darkness called as the pain intensified.

My throat burned from the acid in my stomach, ravaging my voice as I weakly called out for help.

I twisted my neck and looked up, seeing the soft stream of warm light radiating from the café window. Still, no one came. My gaze shifted, and I cried out in horror. Only a few feet away from me was the sightless gaze of my bodyguard. His face was frozen in a grotesque mask of shock.

Before the second kick came, Kiyoshi intervened. "Hiroto, stop. We need her alive. Get her in the car."

The man reached down and lifted me up by my hair.

Again, Kiyoshi admonished him. "Hiroto, don't make me warn you again."

He released me.

My head bounced on the pavement, sending sparks of light behind my eyelids.

This time, he lifted me up in his arms.

It wasn't like when Maxim held me. As scary and as gruff as Maxim could be, I always felt safe and protected in his arms. In Hiroto's arms, I felt cold and scared.

He carried me over to the black sedan. The trunk popped open. Instinctively, I lifted my left arm to push against his chest and get away from him, but my arm wouldn't move. They unceremoniously dumped me into the trunk. They tossed two objects in on top of me, then they closed the lid.

The interior was dark and smelled like tire rubber and gasoline. He had placed me on my left side, so I wasn't able to move my arm to shift my position. They'd wedged me between a tire and the taillights of the car. The engine started, and the car pulled away from the curb.

I knew in movies when a character was in the trunk of a car, they listened for clues to tell them where they were going. All I heard were the sounds of traffic and city life. In the movies there were usually bridges and tolls and fucking fog horns.

I shifted again, trying to take the pressure off my arm, which had gone completely numb. I tried to wiggle my fingers but couldn't even tell if they were moving. They certainly didn't feel like they were. As I shifted, something heavy and soft slid over my hip to land in front of me. I moved my right arm and felt for what had fallen.

It was my purse! I reached inside and found the gun. I quickly buried it inside my makeup bag. I knew better than to pull the gun on them the moment they opened the trunk. I wouldn't know where I was or who I would be facing. It was better to keep it hidden until the time was right.

As the minutes lengthened and the car traveled on, the pain became too much. The darkness and thin oxygen inside the trunk lulled me. My eyelids fell.

My last thought was of Maxim.

Maxim would find me. Of that I had no doubt. He would come for me. It was strange to be so certain of a man I had just met, but there it was. I knew deep in my heart, without a doubt, that Maxim would move heaven and hell to find me and punish those who had hurt me.

As my head fell to the side and consciousness slipped away, I didn't pray to God.

I prayed to Maxim.

CHAPTER 28

axim

DYLAN WOULD NOT BE CONSOLED.

Her beautiful face was a mask of raw pain and fear. Tears streamed down her cheeks as she clutched at Ivan and cried. Never in my life had I seen my friend look so helpless. He clung to her, holding her close as he whispered soothing words in Russian. He placed a hand around the back of her neck and held her against his chest. He then looked over the top of her head at me.

His gaze reflected my own emotions.

I wanted to rage and scream and cry out just like Dylan, but I couldn't afford to.

Carinna needed me to stay calm.

If I gave in to my own feelings of rage and helplessness and guilt, I would be useless to her.

But I felt all those things.

They scratched and clawed from deep inside my chest.

I was a beast blinded by fury and a driving need for vengeance.

I would find these yakuza bastards and make them wish they were never born. Anyone could kill someone, but only the Russians had perfected true torturous pain. It came from generations of eking out a bare living from the hard, frozen ground. From centuries of battling bears, frozen tundra, foreign enemies, and corruption from within. A Russian did not wince in the face of danger, and he never let his enemies off lightly. You only truly defeated an enemy when they had felt your wrath through the generations to come. When you had poisoned their fertile ground and then pissed on it as you left.

They had taken her.

They had taken my babygirl.

Moya lyubimaya.

My beloved.

The woman I loved. Yes, loved. I didn't give a damn that I had only known her for a few days. How long did it take to know someone was your perfect match? To know that someone brought a spark of life and light into your world? To know that you would rather die than think of spending one minute on this earth without them?

In just the span of those same few short days, Carinna had become my oxygen. My reason. My life. She was fun and outspoken and sexy and driven and ambitious and sweet and funny. The hours I'd spent with her were some of the best moments of my life. Unlike with other women, who I'd frequently hastened away from the moment we had slaked our lust, I wanted to linger with Carinna. I wanted to hold her close each night and wake up and sip coffee with her in the morning. I wanted to tease her about her taste in cars and have her tease me about my expensive suits. I wanted to watch her bake bread and savor the warmth of it in my mouth when she gave me a coveted bite. I wanted to see the joy leap into her eyes the moment she saw the sign over her first bakery and be there for her when her first customer came through the door. I wanted to see her hold my children to her breast and hold her hand when they went off on their own. I wanted to share her triumphs and lessen her failures.

I wanted more than just her… I wanted a *life* with her.

And more than anything in the world, I wanted to have her in my arms in this moment so I could tell her I loved her.

The idea that she may die at the hands of my enemies without knowing she was deeply loved pained my soul.

She would not die.

I would find her.

If it took burning this fucking city to the ground—I would find her.

Dylan crumpled to the floor, and Ivan followed her. Cradling her in his arms, he pushed her hair back. "Baby, I need you to talk to me. Please, baby. We need your help."

Dylan sniffed and swiped at her cheeks. "Tell me what I can do."

Not wanting to startle her, I went down on my haunches a few feet away. I kept my voice as soft and low as I could, not wanting her to hear the desperation I felt. "Just tell us about your conversation with Carinna."

Dylan sniffed again.

Ivan gave her a kiss on the forehead.

She seemed to draw strength from his presence. If I hadn't been going through the same thing with Carinna, I would have scoffed at the idea of my cold-hearted friend finding love and companionship so quickly with this small slip of an American girl. Yet, somehow, these two female friends had done the impossible. They had domesticated two hard, set-in-their-ways Russian men.

Dylan inhaled deeply. "We were on the phone talking about her pastry class when a man interrupted."

I leaned in. She continued, "I overheard him say that he owned a restaurant and wanted to hire Carinna as a pastry cook."

"How did he know she was a pastry cook?"

"We had been talking about her looking for a new job. She didn't want to tend bar anymore. Now that she had a few semesters of training, she was going to try for a pastry position at a restaurant."

I couldn't help but smile. My beautiful, stubborn little spitfire. No matter how many times I told her I had plenty of money to support her, she still was insisting on paying her own way.

Ivan stroked Dylan's hair. "Can you remember anything about how he sounded?"

Dylan thought for a moment. "He was soft-spoken, and the café was loud, but I think he may have been Asian. He had a way of emphasizing the last consonants of each word. It was also in how he said the word 'fortuitous.' I don't know, I just remember thinking he sounded Asian and wondering if he owned that amazing Asian restaurant a few blocks away from the café called The Red Dragon and how lucky Carinna would be to get a job there."

Dylan buried her head in Ivan's chest and cried again.

There was a discreet knock on the hotel room door before it opened. Luka walked in. His face was grave. He motioned with his head. I followed him out into the hall and closed the door.

"They found Boris with a gunshot wound to his chest."

I clenched my jaw. "Where?"

"Three blocks down from her apartment. I'm having the boys break into any business along the route with a security camera outside to grab the footage."

"This was Kiyoshi. You know it."

He nodded and placed his hand on my shoulder. "And he's going to die, painfully, for it."

"We have to find him first."

Luka smiled at me. It did not reach his eyes. "And that, my friend, is my specialty."

"We should start with her cell phone. Dimitri has already placed a few phone calls to our contacts within the force."

Dimitri was working that angle as he was leaving town with Emma and their new baby girl, as well as Vaska's wife, Mary. We weren't taking any more chances with the women we loved.

Luka nodded. "I also have some of our men rattling the cages of different contacts around the city. We'll flush the rats out soon."

We both returned to the room. Ivan set Dylan away so he could rise. I held up my hand to stay him. "Don't. Stay here. Carinna may find a way to contact Dylan."

"Are you sure?" asked Ivan, although it was clear he didn't want to leave Dylan in her current state.

"I'm sure, my friend."

I turned to leave.

Dylan's tearstained face looked at me from over Ivan's shoulder. "Please find her. You don't know. You don't know how much she means to me. You have to find her."

"I will. You have my word."

And not even God would save the man who took her.

CHAPTER 29

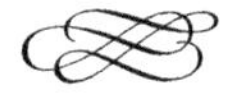

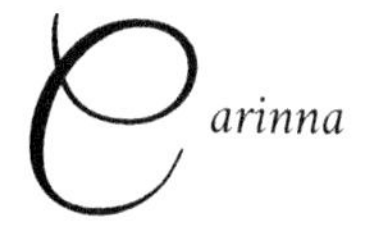*arinna*

PAIN.

That's all I felt.

Pain.

I tried to focus on my surroundings. It didn't feel like I was still in the car's trunk. I shifted. I was lying on some kind of mat or thin mattress by the feel of it. The air was sour like rancid fish. I furrowed my brow as I struggled to open my eyes. When I finally did, it didn't seem to make a difference. I was surrounded by pitch black.

I tried to move my left arm. A shock of pain jolted up over my shoulder and down my spine. I must have dislocated it when I was shoved against that building. The only thing I knew about dislocated shoulders was if you waited too long, nerve damage could set in along the arm and hand. My stomach twisted. As frightening as that was, the use of my hand would be the least of my worries if I were killed.

I needed to get the fuck out of here.

First, I needed to find my purse. Maybe I'd gotten lucky, and they'd tossed my purse and my backpack in here with me.

I hissed air through my clenched jaw as I struggled to sit up. My eyes were slowly adjusting to the light. It looked like I was in some kind of abandoned warehouse. There were dirty cement floors and large wooden columns. The windows were small and high off the ground. The only light in the room was filtered through the individual panes, which were covered in soot and grime.

Tamping down my revulsion, I swept my right hand around my body, searching in the darkness for my purse.

My hand drifted over something soft and warm.

It moved.

I screamed and scurried backward till my body slammed against one of the columns. A chain rattled along the cement floor as it tugged against my ankle. Fuck, I was chained. Someone chained me here beside something that just moved. A rat?

There was a low groan.

It sounded like a woman.

I swallowed several times. Trying to get some moisture back into my chalk-like mouth. "Hello?"

No answer.

"Is someone there?"

There was another low groan.

Then the rattle of another chain.

Whoever it was, someone had also chained them up.

I squinted into the darkness, desperately trying to see.

Finally, someone spoke. "Hello?" The voice was raspy and low as if they hadn't used it in awhile, but I could tell it was a woman.

"My name is Carinna. Who are you?"

There was a long silence. For a moment, I thought she might not respond.

After a long pause, she spoke. "Katie. My name is Katie."

"How long have you been here, Katie?"

I heard her shift position. "What day is it?"

I placed a hand over my upper left arm and rubbed it, trying to get some feeling back into the limb. "If that's sunlight and not streetlights, I think it might be Thursday morning."

The chain rattled again as Katie must have moved. I could barely make out her form in the dim light. She looked small, like a huddled-over rag doll.

"They brought me here, I think, two nights ago. I've been trying to listen for the sound of the birds in the morning to keep track of the days. I don't know where here is, but they kidnapped me, I think, over a week ago, in Virginia."

Her words were uttered calmly, with no emotion. I wasn't sure whether to be impressed or terrified. She was either the most calm, cool, and collected person under fire I'd ever met, or they had beaten the will and fight out of her. "We're in Chicago." I shook my head as I rubbed my temple. "Or at least I was in Chicago. I'm not sure how far we traveled after I blacked out."

Katie's chain rattled as she shifted closer. Her hand landed on my leg, then my hand. She held my hand and then pressed something into it. It was a plastic water bottle. "Here. Drink."

"I can't take this from you. What if—"

"I insist. Whatever their plans, they don't want us dead. They don't feed me often, but they do at least give me some food and enough water to stay alive. Drink. You'll need your strength. Are you injured?"

"I think I dislocated my shoulder. Do you know who took us?"

"The yakuza."

"The what?"

"The yakuza. They are a powerful Japanese crime syndicate."

"What would the yakuza want with me?" I asked.

"I don't know what they want with you, but I'm pretty sure I'm in this mess because of my family."

"Who is your family?"

"The Novikoffs."

She said that like I was supposed to recognize the name, as if she had said the Kennedys or Kardashians. One thing I recognized was it sounded Russian.

"Is that Russian?"

She shifted again, this time to move closer to me. She sat next to me and sighed. "As Russian as they come."

Russian. I hadn't wanted to think about it, but it was hard not to believe that Maxim was somehow responsible for all this. I mean, when I'd said the man was dangerous, I meant to my heart, not to my freaking life! What the hell?

Dangerous.

That's right, Maxim was dangerous. Pretty fucking dangerous just by the look of him. Maxim was going to find me and make these assholes pay. I knew it deep in my bones. I just had to stay alive until then. I patted Katie's leg. "Don't worry. My boyfriend, Maxim, will find us."

My stomach gave a little schoolgirl flip when I called him my boyfriend, which was insane, of course, considering I was currently chained to a fucking wall.

Katie sat up a little straighter. "Maxim? Maxim Konatantinovich Miloslavsky? He's in Chicago?"

My stomach now did a schoolgirl 'stay the fuck away from my boyfriend' jealous clench.

My eyes narrowed. "Yes. You know Maxim?"

Although I couldn't see it, I heard the smile in her voice. "Yes, I know Maxim. I was there when he got his piercing."

My mouth dropped open on a gasp.

"Oh, God! No! Not *that* piercing, the other ones. Although, I thought *that* piercing was just a rumor."

"No, it's very real. So you and Maxim were… friends?"

I held my breath, waiting for her response. If I had to die, I'd rather not die chained to a former girlfriend of the man I loved.

Fuck. Loved! Loved? I just thought about the word love. First boyfriend and now love. Trauma can do crazy things to your mind. A life-or-death situation certainly had a way of putting things into perspective. Gone were all the doubts about how our lifestyles were incompatible or how I hadn't known him for very long or how he was too intense and controlling.

All that just floated away to reveal the one kernel of truth left remaining. I loved him. I loved how he winked at me when he was trying to get his way. How he talked dirty to me in the bedroom. How he held me close as we slept. How he defended me to my parents. How he showed an interest in my bakery business plan. I even loved how he kneaded bread! I was in love with the arrogant, insufferable man.

Katie laughed. "Hell, no. He's a little too laid-back for my taste. Besides, he's Russian. I promised myself I would never date a Russian."

Too laid-back? Jesus, what was her type? The damn Hulk?

She continued, her voice filling the dark void. "We hung out together when he was working with the Ivanovs a few years ago. I had wanted to get my nipples pierced, but was worried it would be painful, so Maxim offered to do it first as a kind of a joke. The moment I saw that piercing gun, I practically passed out and never went through with it."

I took another tiny sip of her water, not wanting to drink

it all. "Well, I'm sure by now he knows I'm missing. It won't be long before he finds us."

She patted my knee. "That's what I thought a week ago. I could have sworn my father would have sent someone to find me. I even thought I overheard them talking about a man tracking them down, but I have to be honest, I was starting to lose hope."

I lifted my good arm around her shoulders. "Don't lose hope. Maxim is going to save us both. I promise. We just have to stick together and stay alive until they do. Any idea why these yakadoodles took us?"

"The yakuza, and from what I've overheard, Kiyoshi is in charge. He's here to establish a guns trade business, but first they have to get rid of the Russians who already have a lock on the market both here and on the East Coast."

"So what does kidnapping us solve?"

"Their plan is to distract the men so they are more focused on finding us than on protecting their business interests. They had planned on grabbing Samara and Yelena. They are the wives of Gregor and Damian Ivanov, but they were too well protected, so they targeted me instead. No one gave a damn about my protection, I guess. Then they came here to grab Emma. She's Dimitri's wife, but she's pregnant right now and they were worried she'd slow them down."

"So they grabbed me instead."

"Bingo."

Well, at least I saved Emma and her baby from this trauma. If they had to grab someone, at least it was me and not her or Mary or, God forbid, Dylan.

I took a deep breath. "Well, that is where they fucked up, because we're going to get out of here."

"We are? Look, I've tried countless times, but—"

"You were alone then. You have me now."

In the burgeoning morning light, I could finally make out

her features. She smiled. She took a fortifying breath. "You're right. We can't let the men have all the glory in rescuing us. These Russian men are far too arrogant as it is. What's your plan?"

"When they dumped me in here, did you happen to see them bring in my purse or backpack?"

She frowned. "It was pitch black, but I heard them put something over there just as they were leaving."

I turned and searched the dark recesses of the warehouse floor. There, several feet away, just out of reach, was a metal folding chair. On it were my purse and backpack.

I pointed to the chair. "That's my purse."

Katie shook her head. "The first thing they would have done was look for your cell phone and tossed it out."

I shook my head. "Yes, but they probably missed the gun hidden in my makeup bag."

CHAPTER 30

Maxim

We were getting close.

Vaska, Luka, and I stood across the street from the last yakuza safehouse. It was isolated on a deserted street, surrounded by half-torn down and boarded up homes. It was the perfect place to hide out and lie low. Located in a rundown, quiet part of Southside Chicago, there were no neighbors or prying eyes.

Over the last eleven hours, we had systematically searched every hole and under every rock to eliminate any yakuza gang members we found in the city. With each house, with each kill, we crept closer to getting to Kiyoshi while weakening his forces. But it was taking too long, it was already dawn. We no longer had the advantage of the cover of night. By now, word would have spread around their organization that we were on the attack. We had to get to Kiyoshi now before he had a chance to move the girls.

"So the intel is good?" I asked Vaska.

He nodded. "Solid. Hiroto is holed up in there right now."

Luka flicked a lighter on and off. "Kiyoshi's right-hand man. He'll know where the girls are being kept."

Vaska shook his head. "The fundamental problem is that's our only intel. We have no idea what the layout of the place is, how it's secured, or how many men he may have in there. We're going in blind."

Luka flicked the lighter on. "Then I say it's time for Plan B."

Vaska smiled. "I like how you think."

I nodded. "Let's do this. They have held Carinna captive for close to twelve hours. I don't want to—"

I couldn't finish the sentence. If I focused on the horrors she may be enduring because of me, I would go mad. I needed to stay focused and find her. There would be plenty of time later, when she was safe, for recriminations and guilt.

Luka placed his hand on my shoulder. "We'll find them both, my friend. Of that you can be certain."

We stepped back into the darkness and headed down the alley where we had parked Vaska's Range Rover. It was completely *murdered* out in matte black paint with no plates. It was the vehicle they used for these covert missions. Opening the back, we pulled out four cans of gasoline. I flanked to the right, and Vaska and Luka flanked to the left. Keeping low, we poured the gasoline around the perimeter of the house, dousing the foundation.

We returned to our positions across the street. Vaska handed us each a water-soaked rag to wipe our hands.

Luka flicked his lighter on.

After only the slightest pause, he dropped it to the ground.

There was a whooshing sound, then a flash of bright orange flame surrounded by a cobalt blue flame rushed in a line from our position straight to the house. The fire line split as it immediately surrounded the house's foundation. Flames licked the walls and thick clouds of black smoke rose into the morning sky. The old, mostly abandoned house went up like a tinderbox.

It only took a few minutes before the front door swung open. A large Japanese man stumbled out of the home, surrounded by a halo of smoke.

He fell down the front steps, rose and then stumbled again, falling to his knees on the pavement as he struggled to breathe.

We walked across the street and stood over him. From the photo we had as a reference, we knew this was Hiroto.

Vaska kicked him. He fell on his back, like the cockroach he was. I then stepped on his chest. His eyes widened as he struggled to breathe. "Tell me where Carinna and Katia are being kept. Now."

"Fuck you," he choked out.

I leaned down on my haunches. Pulling my gun free from my back holster, I pushed the barrel into Hiroto's mouth. I then calmly threatened, "I will blow your teeth through the back of your motherfucking brain."

Hiroto's teeth clattered against the metal barrel as he started rapidly talking, diming out his boss.

CHAPTER 31

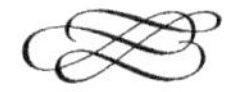

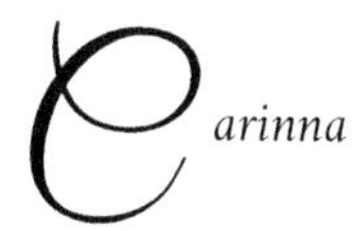arinna

"Fuck, so close!"

"Try again," said Katie.

She was stretched out on the flimsy mattress with her leg extended as far as it would go. We realized her chain was slightly longer and closer to the chair than mine. Using my good arm, I swung the chain along the floor again, trying to hook the metal chair's leg.

This time the chain hit, causing a loud clang, but didn't catch.

We both stilled.

Holding our breaths, we listened for any sign or cry of alarm. After several seconds, we breathed easier. I hadn't seen or heard from our captors since I regained consciousness. Katie said it wasn't unusual to not see them for an entire day or so.

Katie shimmied back into position. I swept the chain

across the floor again. This time it caught the leg. Only a few links were wrapped around it, but it might be enough.

Wincing as I put pressure on my arm, I leaned down onto my stomach. I carefully pulled on the chain until it was taut. The chair shifted toward us a few inches.

"It's working!" exclaimed Katie.

I pressed my palm against the chain, not daring to even lift it up, and pulled it toward me again.

The chair shifted some more.

The next time I pulled on the chain, the chair shifted, but several links shifted as well, almost breaking its grasp on the leg.

Fuck.

I leaned up on my elbows so I could suck in a deep breath before I once more laid flat on the dirty mattress. If I could just get the chair a little bit closer before the link unraveled. I pulled on it again. Another link slipped. I stopped. We held our breath. I pulled again. The chair inched closer. Then again. Inch by painstaking inch, the chair moved closer to us. When the link fell off the chair leg, it was close enough for me to easily swing the chain along the floor and wrap it around the leg more securely. The second the chair was within reach, we grabbed for it. I snatched my purse off the seat and rummaged for the makeup bag. As I lifted it, I almost cried with relief. The makeup bag was heavy and overstuffed, which meant the gun must still be inside.

"Watch the door," I called out to Katie as I unzipped the bag.

The barrel was covered in pressed powder and some smears from one of my lipsticks that lost its cap, but it was there. I pulled it free.

Katie looked down at the gun. "What now?"

"Now? Now we wait. Eventually, someone will return to give us food. When they do, we'll shoot them, grab the keys, and escape. Maybe we'll get lucky and they'll have the keys to a car too, or at least a cell phone, so we can call the cops."

"No. No cops."

I raised an eyebrow.

"You're new to the Russian way," she said. "No cops. Ever. We'll call Maxim. You already said he's out there looking for you."

My cheeks heated. "I don't know his number."

"I know Gregor's number. We'll call him." Katie lifted the chain. "Or we could fire a bullet into the chains and try to escape ourselves?"

I bit my lip. Both were good plans. "I only just learned to fire a gun. I don't know if I would hit the chain or wind up blowing my own leg off."

Katie grimaced. "I'm a terrible shot. Like really, really terrible."

I took a deep breath and thought for a moment. "Okay, we wait a few more hours. If someone doesn't come, then we try shooting through the chains. That way, if we are successful, we can escape under the cover of darkness. It might give us an advantage."

Katie nodded. "Good plan."

We leaned against the wall and hid the gun between us. Katie took a sip from her water bottle and handed it to me.

Then we waited.

And waited.

Neither of us spoke for what seemed like hours. I wasn't sure if it was nerves, or we had decided by quiet, mutual consent to conserve our energy, or just plain fear.

We watched as the light slowly dimmed. The sun was setting. It was almost time.

I tightened my right arm across my stomach as it growled. The first thing I would do when I got free was to eat an entire pizza with extra sausage and black olives on my own. At least my left arm had mostly stopped hurting. Now there was just this dull ache. I was fairly certain that was a terrible sign, but there was no point in dwelling on it now.

I swallowed, trying to moisten my dry mouth. "I think we need to try shooting through the chains."

Katie nodded. "I'll push my chain out as far as possible and you try to shoot it."

"Me? Why me?"

"Because it's your gun."

"Yeah, but it's your plan."

"I don't think I've explained just how bad of a shot I am."

I exhaled in a huff. "Well, Maxim did say I was a good shot."

Katie leaned over to push the chain as far away from us as possible. "Tag, you're it then."

I picked up the gun. Instinctively, I went to raise my left arm to grip it with both hands, but my arm wouldn't budge. "Wait! I can't hold it with both hands."

"You'll be fine. It's just a small revolver. They don't have that bad of a kick."

Katie leaned back behind me.

I raised the gun and aimed the barrel at the chain. "Are you ready?"

She squeezed my upper arm in encouragement. "You can do this, Carinna. Just imagine Kiyoshi's face."

I pulled back the hammer and re-aimed. I inhaled. Then exhaled, just like Maxim taught me.

Right before I pressed the trigger, there was a commotion outside the door at the other end of the warehouse floor. The heavy metal door swung open, banging against the wall. Kiyoshi appeared along with three brutish-looking men.

Katie quickly placed her hand on the gun and lowered it, hiding my arm between the two of our bodies.

Kiyoshi looked like a man possessed. Gone was the calm

demeanor and expensive suit. His trouser pants were wrinkled, and his shirt was dirty and untucked. He waved a gun about as he started shouting at us in Japanese.

Katie leaned in close. "Wait. Wait till he gets closer. We can't risk you missing."

With a start, I realized she expected me to shoot him. To shoot another human being. To wait until he got closer, so I'd be more likely to hit and kill him. My whole body went rigid. Could I kill another human being?

Kiyoshi and his men were now halfway across the bare warehouse floor.

"Almost there," whispered Katie over my shoulder. "Steady. Steady. Aim for Kiyoshi."

Even if by some miracle I hit Kiyoshi, we would still need to worry about the other three men. There was no fucking way I was going to somehow summon my inner Rambo and be able to hit all four in rapid succession. Still, hitting Kiyoshi, cutting off the head of the snake, might make the others run away. I mean, that's what they did in the movies. Right? It could work.

I rubbed my sweaty palm on my jeans and gripped the gun's handle again. I could hear Maxim's voice in my head. *You can do this, babygirl.*

"Now!" yelled Katie.

I raised the gun and aimed for Kiyoshi.

At the last second, I squeezed my eyes shut and fired, opening my eyes to look only when the blast of the bullet leaving the chamber jarred my arm. The bullet skimmed Kiyoshi's head and landed in the metal door behind him… a few inches away from Maxim's stunned face.

CHAPTER 32

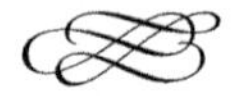

Maxim

NOT THE WELCOME I was expecting, but certainly the one I deserved.

I shifted to the right just in time as a bullet lodged in the door a scant two inches away from my head. I looked up to see Carinna's shocked face.

Thank God, my beautiful babygirl was alive.

And judging by the gun in her hand, my little spitfire was still fighting for her life.

But now it was my turn.

Luka and I crossed the threshold.

Kiyoshi and three of his men turned.

I slapped my fist against my palm. "Four against two hardly seems fair... for them."

Luka said, "Five, if you count your girl. Whose side is she on, anyway?"

I gave him a side-eye. "Shut the fuck up and let's kill these bastards."

The whole warehouse floor was solid concrete. We couldn't risk firing our weapons. A ricochet could bounce and hit one of the girls. So it looked like I was going to have the pleasure of beating Kiyoshi to death with my fists.

Kiyoshi and two of his men charged us, firing wildly in our direction. Luka and I ran straight into the line of fire, knowing we had to get the guns away from them. The second Kiyoshi got close, I landed a kick to his groin and then slammed the palm of my hand against his inner wrist, forcing him to drop his weapon.

I ducked his first swing and landed a fist in his kidneys. He rebounded with a sideswipe kick, knocking me to the ground. He landed another kick straight in my ribs. I both heard and felt the moment at least two of them cracked. Using my upper body weight, I leapt to my feet and punched Kiyoshi in the stomach, then the jaw. He staggered back. I punched him again in the face, feeling his cheekbone break beneath my knuckles. He fell to the floor, motionless.

I knew he wasn't dead.

I didn't want him dead.

That would come later... much later.

There would be no such thing as a quick and painless death for him. He would suffer and suffer greatly before we shipped his body back to Japan, piece by piece. The yakuza were going to get the message to never fuck with us again. It was one thing to go after us and to try to steal our business. It brought on a whole different level of hellish consequences when you went after our women.

Luka took on the second guy with a heavy fist to the jaw, knocking him unconscious.

There was a second gunshot. Alarmed, I scanned the place. Carinna was standing with the gun pointed at the floor. There was a puff of smoke rising from the cement and a broken chain at her feet.

The bastards had chained my girl to the wall. I growled as I turned to face the third man, ready to rip his head clean off his body.

Then I heard Carinna scream.

The fourth man had her in a chokehold from behind. Katie had leapt onto his back and was using the chain from around her ankle to choke him in return.

Luka shouted, "I got him. Help the girls."

I ran the length of the warehouse, getting to the girls the moment the fourth man threw Katie off. She went flying a few feet backward, slamming against the wall and slowly sliding to the floor. Without the weight on his back, the fourth man increased the pressure around Carinna's neck.

With a roar, I grabbed him by the shoulders and pulled him off her. Carinna fell to her knees, choking and gasping. In a rage, I pounded my fists into the man's face. Blood burst from his nose and coated his teeth. Finally, he fell limp.

I turned to comfort Carinna, but she wasn't there.

In a panic, I scanned the dimly lit warehouse floor.

Carinna screamed again. "You piece of shit asshole!"

Kiyoshi had come to his senses and was crawling to the exit. Carinna had run over to him and landed a few well-placed kicks to his midsection.

He curled up into the fetal position as he held his arms over his face. "Get her off me!"

"Fuck you!" cried Carinna as she kicked him in the ribs again.

As much as I would have loved to watch my girl kick the shit out of Kiyoshi, I needed to make sure she was okay.

Ignoring the pain in my side from my broken ribs, I pulled Carinna off Kiyoshi and hugged her to my chest. Cradling her head against the crook of my arm, I had to fight back the tears that clouded my vision. "Jesus Christ, you scared me, babygirl. Don't ever do that again."

She tilted her head back. Tears streamed down her cheeks. "Don't do what? Get kidnapped against my will?" she quipped. I knew she couldn't be too hurt if she still had that sassy, smart-ass tongue of hers that I loved.

I swiped the sides of my thumbs over her cheeks, wiping away the tears. "Yeah, that."

She laid her cheek against my heart. "Okay." Then she tilted her head back again. "Unless it's by you, right?"

I laughed through my tears, and I hugged her body close. "Yes, babygirl, unless it's by me."

The adrenaline that had kept her going through the entire ordeal wore off. I could feel the impact of the trauma race over her limbs as her entire body shook and trembled.

She fisted my shirt. "Am I safe now? Is it over?"

I stroked her hair as I continued to hold her tight. "Yes, *moya lyubimaya,* it's over. You're safe. No one's ever going to hurt you again, baby. I swear."

She nodded as her grip slackened. "Good," she said weakly, "because I think I'm going to—"

Her head fell back as her body went limp. She had fainted.

I bent down to swipe her legs under her knees and lift her into my arms. The piece of chain that was still attached to her ankle rattled. My stomach twisted and bile rose in the back of my throat. The very first thing I was going to do when I got her out of here was take that motherfucking chain off her.

"Careful of her arm," called out Katie.

"What's wrong with her arm?" I asked as I held her gently, scanning her for injuries.

"She dislocated her left shoulder trying to fight them off," responded Katie from her seated position against the wall.

I kissed Carinna's forehead. "That's my little spitfire, *moya malen'kaya iskra*. Don't worry, I'm here now."

There was another gunshot. This time, it was Luka breaking Katie's chain.

He then went down on his haunches and attempted to lift her into his arms. "My name is Luka. Your father sent me to find you, Katia."

She batted his arms away. "It's Katie and I don't need your help."

Katie scrambled to her knees and braced a palm against the wall as she struggled to rise. The moment she did, her knees buckled. Luka was there to catch her. Against her protests, he lifted her into his arms and made his way back to us.

"Put me down!" ordered Katie.

Luka responded with a grin, *"Izvini. Ya ne govoryu po-angliyski"*

Katie fumed as she crossed her arms and tried to keep her body from pressing against his. "You do too speak English, you big gorilla. *A teper' opusti menya!*"

Luka's eyebrow rose. "So the little Russian princess remembers her mother tongue."

Katie's lips thinned as she turned her head and refused to speak to him any further, but not without first muttering under her breath in a different language, *"Gorille stupide."*

Luka tightened his grasp. *"Je parle français aussi, princesse."*

Katie flashed him a disgruntled look as he carried her over the threshold.

I followed with an unconscious Carinna in my arms.

Our men would pick up Kiyoshi and his men and take them to our warehouse, where their real nightmare would begin.

But that was for later. For now, Carinna was my only priority.

CHAPTER 33

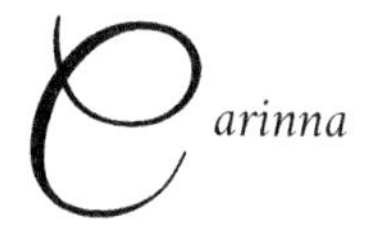

arinna

I OPENED MY EYES, but then quickly shut them against the bright fluorescent lights. Squinting, I tried opening them again. I scanned the room. Judging by the white walls and thin knit blanket over my body, I was in a hospital bed.

I looked down to see Maxim.

He had pulled up a chair close to my bed and was holding my hand as he rested his head. He was sound asleep. I'd never watched him in his sleep. He didn't look peaceful. His brow was furrowed, and his cheeks were hollow, as if he hadn't truly slept or eaten in days. His usually clean-shaven cheeks were rough with stubble. Gone was his customary expensive suit. He was in a pair of jeans and just a simple, wrinkled black T-shirt.

I looked down at our joined hands. His large and tanned, covered in tattoos. Mine pale and small. A complete mismatch, and yet they fit perfectly.

Maxim stirred.

His emerald gaze focused on me. You could see the moment his fitful sleep faded and reality set in.

He sat up straighter. "You're awake."

I went to respond, but it came out as more of a croak. My throat was so dry.

Maxim rose and scooped some ice chips from a bucket into a cup. "Here you go. Just one at a time." He held a chip to my lips, tracing the outline and leaving a cool shimmer of water on them before slipping it into my mouth.

He then sat down.

"I'm dying," I said.

His eyes widened. "What? No, baby, you're fine. They had to reset your shoulder, but there is no lasting nerve damage. It will just be sore for a little while and you'll have to wear the sling for a week or two."

I shook my head. "No. I must be dying, either that or you don't want me anymore."

His gaze heated. "How could you ever think that?"

"You just slipped a piece of ice in my mouth without the slightest sexual innuendo. So either I'm dying or you are, but one of us is dying."

He sat down and grasped my hand again. He held it up to his lips. Then pressed it against his cheek. "I almost lost you. All this pain. It's my fault. If you hadn't met me—"

"You were looking after me. Protecting me. I am sure if you had it to do all over again, you'd make the same decision, knowing that no matter what happened, in the end I was safe and that was all that mattered. Sound familiar? Your words. That is what you told me about my brother. Well, the same applies to us. Bad things happen. They shouldn't outweigh the good. Are you saying you would have preferred to never have met me at all?"

"No, babygirl, no. I love you. No matter what, I'll never regret meeting you."

"You love me?"

Maxim smirked. "Baby, a man like me does not buy groceries, play chauffeur, and hang out in pastry classes for a woman he doesn't love."

I played with the edge of my blanket. "When were you planning on telling me?"

He threw up his hands and shook his head. "Oh, this is exactly how I planned to tell the first woman that I've ever loved, that I love her. A nice romantic meal of ice chips in a sterile hospital room."

My brow furrowed. "First woman? First woman!"

He wrapped his hand around my neck and pulled me in for a hard kiss. "First, last, and only woman."

I pouted. "That's better."

He looked at me and raised an eyebrow. "Don't you have something to say back to me?"

I stretched out my good arm and tucked my fingers behind my head. "Nope."

"Nope?"

I shook my head, giving him a cheeky grin. "Nope. I think I'm going to make you sweat it out a little longer. I mean, you did get me kidnapped and all."

Maxim's face clouded over.

I grimaced. "Too soon to joke about it?"

"Way too soon," he growled.

He was probably right. I was sure it was just the pain meds and leftover adrenaline pumping in my veins that was leading to my upbeat cavalier attitude. I didn't care. There would be plenty of time for the trauma and anxiety over what had happened to hit me, especially dealing with my guilt over getting my bodyguard killed. I knew that from experience after my brother's death. At least this time, I knew that Maxim would be there to chase away the demons and make sure I felt safe again.

Maxim leaned down and gave me a kiss on the forehead. "You should rest."

There was a sadness in the dark green depths of his eyes. I reached out and grasped his hand. "You know I was just teasing? You know I love you too?"

He stroked my cheek. "*Moya lyubimaya,* know that whatever happens, that I love you more than my life. Now rest."

With that, he left the room.

My stomach twisted in knots. What did he mean by *whatever happens*?

CHAPTER 34

axim

I CLOSED Carinna's hospital room door and nodded toward Vaska. "Did you get it?"

Vaska and Mary approached. He handed me a large manila envelope. "Everything you asked for."

I opened the envelope and slid the contents into my hand. There was a pair of new car keys, a bank statement, mortgage statement, and several credit cards.

Vaska sighed. "This is a mistake, my friend."

I refused to listen. The moment I had Carinna squared away with the doctors, I'd instructed Vaska to get Carinna a new car and to sign over one of our properties in her name. I then had him transfer my portion of our recent gun buy, two million dollars, into a bank account in her name as well. They listed me as a co-owner on the account so I could transfer more money into it whenever she was low on funds. As far as I was concerned, she would never have to worry about money again. She would also never have to worry about being put into danger because I was getting out of her life.

I shook my head. "It is the only way I can keep her safe."

Mary placed a hand on my upper arm. "She's safer with you."

"That is not true. This never would have happened if it hadn't been for me and the life I lead. I can't put her in that kind of danger again."

Mary crossed her arms over her chest and huffed. "Don't you think you should let her decide that? It is her life too."

"No, she will only say she wants to stay with me. I can't allow that."

Vaska placed a protective arm around Mary's waist. "Mary is right. Your woman is stronger than you think."

"My mind is made up. Is the plane ready?"

Knowing he would not change my mind, Vaska nodded. "It's waiting for you in the private hangar at Midway."

"Good. I have a few loose ends to tie up and then I'm headed back to Moscow tonight."

Vaska knew the loose ends were Kiyoshi and his men, but we would not discuss that in the public corridor of a hospital. "Ivan is already at the warehouse. I'll walk you out and we can discuss what to do with the bodies. Mary—"

Mary gave Vaska a kiss on the cheek. "I'll watch over Carinna. I know Dylan is already on her way over."

Vaska smiled. He pointed to the two guards who were standing a discreet distance away. "Remember, these are your guards, not your delivery boys. Do not send them to the vending machines for Doritos. Their job is to guard you, not fetch for you."

She rolled her eyes.

I watched the exchange and felt a heavy weight of sorrow fall on my shoulders. I wanted this. I wanted what they had.

This fun banter and camaraderie with the woman I loved. I breathed deeply. I took one more glance at Carinna through the hospital room door window.

She looked so peaceful, and the only way she would stay that way was if I got out of her life as soon as possible.

I placed a hand on Vaska's shoulder. "Goodbye, my friend. Watch over her for me."

Vaska nodded.

I turned and left, refusing to allow myself even one more glance back at the future I could have had.

CHAPTER 35

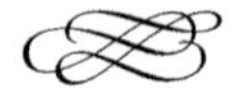

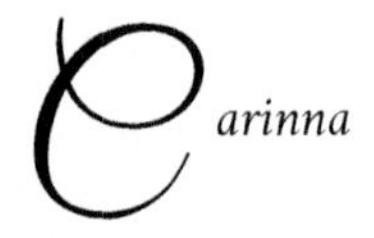

Carinna

"WAKE UP!"

I blinked.

"Wake up, Carinna!"

I opened my eyes and frowned, confused as to why Mary was leaning over my bed yelling at me.

"What's going on?"

Mary rifled through the plastic bag that held my belongings, which the nurse had placed on the chair near my bed. "He's leaving, that's what's going on."

I frowned as I pushed myself to a seated position with my good arm. "Who's leaving?"

"Maxim."

"What do you mean, Maxim's leaving?"

Mary let out a frustrated sigh as she pulled out my jeans and gave them a shake before holding them up. "He's getting on a plane to Moscow in a few hours and leaving, because like a typical stupid boy he thinks that is what's best for you. Now get up." She pulled the blanket off me.

What the fuck? He couldn't say he loved me and then just have left!

"That bastard!" I exclaimed as I swung my legs over the edge of the bed.

Mary's lips twisted in a smirk. "My thoughts exactly. But don't worry. We will not let him get away with it."

With my arm in a sling, I needed Mary's help to get into my jeans and shoes. She returned to the plastic bag and pulled out my T-shirt. Unfortunately, not only was it filthy, the hospital staff had also cut it in half when they treated my dislocated shoulder. She shook her head. "Well, this won't work." She tossed the T-shirt aside and unbuttoned her black cardigan. It was an adorable sweater with little pink cats with crystals for eyes on it.

"I can't take your sweater!"

"Sure you can. Now get out of that hospital gown. We don't have much time, Vaska will be back soon and he'll freak out if he knew what I was doing right now."

I tore off my gown and Mary helped me gingerly put my injured arm through the sleeve, button it back up, then put the sling back on.

Mary put on the hospital gown and buckled her black, wide belt around her waist. She then bloused up the top. She raised her arms. "See? I can make anything look good," she said with a saucy wink. Damn if she wasn't right.

Mary handed me her purse. "Take it. It has the keys to my car. It's the lipstick red Mustang in parking lot B. You can't miss it. My phone passcode is 0119. I peeked at Vaska's phone and grabbed all of Maxim's contact information and uploaded it into mine. There's also money in the wallet, just in case. Head to private hangar C-2 at Midway Airport. I'll tell the pilot to let you on the plane."

We crept over to the door.

I looked at Mary. "Am I allowed to just leave? I think they make you sign papers and stuff first."

She laughed and patted me on the cheek. "Aw, sweetie. You're so cute. Don't worry. You'll get used to dating a Russian criminal. There is no such thing as official paperwork. As far as the hospital is concerned, you were never here. Now wait one moment."

Mary opened the door and sauntered out into the hallway. She spoke in rapid Russian to the two guards and motioned wildly with her hands. They looked confused at first, but then ran down the hallway.

Mary returned to me.

"What did you say to them?"

She shrugged. "I ordered them to go find a vending machine with Doritos for me. Now you have to go."

I scurried a few steps down the hallway and then turned. "Thank you!"

She waved me off. "Make sure you invite me to the wedding."

I walked as fast as I dared without drawing attention to myself until I found an elevator to the parking garage.

How dare he think he could pull my hair, spank my ass, call me pretty, and tell me he loved me and then just waltz out of my life all because of a little kidnapping! Well, Maxim Konatantinovich Miloslavsky was about to find out that he had just met his match—and as he was so fond of saying to me, *I wasn't so easy to get rid of!*

CHAPTER 36

axim

I CLIMBED the stairs leading to the plane's cabin, then tossed my black duffle bag on the nearest seat and headed to the bar. I stepped behind the small counter and reached for the vodka. My plan was to get completely shit-faced drunk on the way back to Moscow. It was the only way I wouldn't break down and tell the pilot to return to Chicago.

"Well, we both know how stubborn he can be."

I stilled. Keeping my grasp on the vodka bottle, I turned to the source of the voice.

Carinna was sitting in one of the large swivel leather chairs on the phone.

My brow furrowed. I slammed the vodka bottle onto the bar. "What the fuck?"

She placed her hand over the mouthpiece and said, "Shhh, language! I'm on the phone." She then returned to her call. "Yes, that was him." She gave me a once-over with that cheeky gaze of hers. "Yes, he is. His cheeks are all red. He looks like he's ready to burst!"

I marched toward her. Placing my hands on my hips, I leaned down. "Carinna, who is that on the phone?"

She once again placed her hand over the mouthpiece. "Your mother."

My eyebrows shot up. "My mother?"

She nodded, then turned her attention back to the call. "No, I think we'll need separate bedrooms, until he makes an honest woman of me, at least."

I ran my hand through my hair. "You're on the phone with *my mother*? How did you get her number?"

She mouthed *Mary*, before saying, "Oh, my God, I would love for you to teach me your recipe for *medovik*! I've always wanted to try baking that traditional honey cake but was worried I'd screw up all the layers."

Taking a deep breath, I tried counting to ten, but only got to three. "Babygirl, give me that phone."

She frowned and stuck her tongue out at me.

I leaned down and growled, "You stick your tongue out at me like that again and I'm going to put that mouth to good use."

Her cheeks glowed a beautiful dark pink. She then stammered into the phone, "No, no, I'm still listening."

My patience was at an end.

I snatched the phone from her grasp. For Carinna's benefit, I stuck to English. "Carinna has to go now, Mama."

I unbuckled my belt with one hand as I raised an eyebrow suggestively. Her eyes widened. "Of course I've told her I love her, Mama."

I whipped the belt free as I kicked off my shoes. I then said through clenched teeth, "In fact, I'm going to show her *just how much I love her* right now."

She slipped out of her seat and tried to run down the

aisle. I caught a fistful of her hair and pulled her back until her body was flush against my chest. "I have to go now, Mama. We'll see you in a few hours. Say bye now, Carinna."

"Bye!" she called out.

I hung up the phone and tossed it aside. I brushed her hair to the side and snarled into her ear, "You are a very bad girl. You're supposed to be recovering at the hospital."

She frowned as she poked me in the chest with her finger. "And you are an arrogant bastard. How dare you tell me you love me and then try sneaking out of the country!"

I slipped my arm around her waist, careful of her sling. I unbuttoned her cardigan. "It was for your own good."

She reached around her hip and ran her hand over my cock, which was straining against my jeans. "I think I'm perfectly capable of deciding what is and isn't for my own good."

I cupped her breast as I licked the side of her neck. "No, you're not."

She sighed as she pushed her ass against my hips. "There's that word again. Don't you know any other answer but no?"

I turned her around in my arms and smoothed her hair away from her face. I placed both of my hands on her pert ass and pulled her as close as possible. "Ask me a question and we'll see."

She licked her lips. "Do you love me?"

"Yes."

"Do you want to be with me?"

"Yes."

"Do you want to marry me?"

I teased her lips with mine. "God, yes."

She leaned in closer. "So it turns out you do know more than one English word."

Remembering the first time we bantered like this, I

smiled. "I know plenty of English words. Lick. Fuck. Wet. Hot. Now it's time to teach you Russian."

I swept her into my arms and carried her to the private bedroom on the plane. I had almost made the biggest mistake of my life. Now that she was in my arms, I was never letting her go.

Carinna nibbled on my ear. "How do you say in Russian, I'm going to punish you, my dirty girl?"

God, I loved this woman.

THE END.

SWEET FEROCITY SNEAK PEEK

Katia stirred in her bed before opening her eyes.

She started and shrank back against the metal headboard. "How did you get in here? The door was locked."

I smirked. "I unlocked it."

She raised her arm and pointed. "If you want your money, it's in the top drawer of my bureau. I only used about seven hundred for an airline ticket and cab ride. I'll pay you back."

I reached for my belt buckle. "Oh princess, it's not the money I want."

She reached for the blanket and pulled it up to cover her chest. "I want you to leave."

I ran my tongue over my bottom lip, then nodded in her direction. "We have unfinished business."

"The hell we do. You rescued me. I'm grateful. You want to get paid? Talk to my father. I have nothing to do with it."

My gaze traveled slowly over her body. "This isn't about your father or the money he owes me. This is about you and me."

Her eye narrowed. "There is no you and me."

"I've had my cock deep inside of you, babygirl. Don't act like there is nothing between us."

She shifted on the bed as she clutched at the blanket. "You don't have to be so coarse. We had sex. That's all. It was no big deal. It didn't mean anything."

I winked as I reached down to grab my hard cock through my jeans. "Oh, trust me, baby, it was a *big* deal, and it did mean something."

She could try and blow it off as nothing, but I didn't believe her. She was a virgin. I was the first man to claim her. The first to feel her tight pussy grip my cock. It fucking meant something — to both of us.

"Well, even if it did, it's over. I don't date Russians. So get out."

I smirked. "It's cute you think all I want to do is date you, and it's far from over, Katia."

"My name is Katie."

"Your name is Katia, and you are as full-blooded Russian as I am. You share the same hot passions and have the same fierce spirit. Stop denying your heritage. Stop denying what's between us."

She dropped the blanket and leaned toward me on her knees. "Are you deaf? There is no us!"

I whipped the belt from my jeans belt loops. "I guess I'm just going to have to prove it to you."

She leaned back. "I'll scream."

I reached behind me and pulled out my Glock and engaged the slide, chambering a bullet. I lifted it high, then placed it within reach on the top of her bureau. "Go ahead. First person through that door gets a bullet between the eyes."

She gasped.

I nodded, "Lay down on your stomach and pull your pajama shorts down."

"You can't be serious."

"Do I look like I'm joking?"

"Luka, I—"

"Do as I say. Now!"

She jumped and slid down the headboard. She turned onto her stomach. Her body stilled.

"Pull down your shorts and panties. Let me see that cute ass of yours."

She sniffed as she swiped at a tear. Her arms trembled as she pushed her silk pajama shorts and a pair of light blue lace panties down to the top of her thighs.

I folded my leather belt in half as I approached the bed. I used it to caress her skin. "You were a very bad girl, Katia. You should not have run away from me like that."

"You didn't give me a choice."

I continued to caress her skin. "You always have a choice. You chose to disobey me. Now you need to be punished. For your own safety, I need you to understand there are consequences for disobedience."

ABOUT ZOE BLAKE

USA TODAY BESTSELLING AUTHOR IN DARK ROMANCE

She delights in writing dark romance books filled with overly possessive billionaires, taboo scenes, and unexpected twists. She usually spends her ill-gotten gains on martinis, travel, and red lipstick. Since she can barely boil water, she's lucky enough to be married to a sexy chef.

ALSO BY ZOE BLAKE

RUTHLESS OBSESSION SERIES

A Dark Mafia Romance

Sweet Cruelty

Dimitri & Emma's story

It was an innocent mistake.

She knocked on the wrong door.

Mine.

If I were a better man, I would've just let her go.

But I'm not.

I'm a cruel bastard.

I ruthlessly claimed her virtue for my own.

It should have been enough.

But it wasn't.

I needed more.

Craved it.

She became my obsession.

Her sweetness and purity taunted my dark soul.

The need to possess her nearly drove me mad.

A Russian arms dealer had no business pursuing a naive librarian student.

She didn't belong in my world.

I would bring her only pain.

But it was too late…

She was mine and I was keeping her.

Sweet Depravity

Vaska & Mary's story

The moment she opened those gorgeous red lips to tell me no, she was mine.

I was a powerful Russian arms dealer and she was an innocent schoolteacher.

If she had a choice, she'd run as far away from me as possible.

Unfortunately for her, I wasn't giving her one.

I wasn't just going to take her; I was going to take over her entire world.

Where she lived.

What she ate.

Where she worked.

All would be under my control.

Call it obsession.

Call it depravity.

I don't give a damn… as long as you call her mine.

Sweet Savagery

Ivan & Dylan's Story

I was a savage bent on claiming her as punishment for her family's mistakes.

As a powerful Russian Arms dealer, no one steals from me and gets away with it.

She was an innocent pawn in a dangerous game.

She had no idea the package her uncle sent her from Russia contained my stolen money.

If I were a good man, I would let her return the money and leave.

If I were a gentleman, I might even let her keep some of it just for frightening her.

As I stared down at the beautiful living doll stretched out before me like a virgin sacrifice,

I thanked God for every sin and misdeed that had blackened my cold heart.

I was not a good man.

I sure as hell wasn't a gentleman… and I had no intention of letting her go.

She was mine now.

And no one takes what's mine.

Sweet Brutality

Maxim & Carinna's story

The more she fights me, the more I want her.

It's that beautiful, sassy mouth of hers.

It makes me want to push her to her knees and dominate her, like the brutal savage I am.

As a Russian Arms dealer, I should not be ruthlessly pursuing an innocent college student like her, but that would not stop me.

A twist of fate may have brought us together, but it is my twisted obsession that will hold her captive as my own treasured possession.

She is mine now.

I dare you to try and take her from me.

Sweet Ferocity

Luka & Katie's Story

I was a mafia mercenary only hired to find her, but now I'm going to keep her.

She is a Russian mafia princess, kidnapped to be used as a pawn in a dangerous territory war.

Saving her was my job. Keeping her safe had become my obsession.

Every move she makes, I am in the shadows, watching.

I was like a feral animal: cruel, violent, and selfishly out for my own needs. Until her.

Now, I will make her mine by any means necessary.

I am her protector, but no one is going to protect her from me.

IVANOV CRIME FAMILY TRILOGY

A Dark Mafia Romance

Savage Vow

Gregor & Samara's story

I took her innocence as payment.

She was far too young and naïve to be betrothed to a monster like me.

I would bring only pain and darkness into her sheltered world.

That's why she ran.

I should've just let her go...

She never asked to marry into a powerful Russian mafia family.

None of this was her choice.

Unfortunately for her, I don't care.

I own her... and after three years of searching... I've found her.

My runaway bride was about to learn disobedience has consequences... punishing ones.

Having her in my arms and under my control had become an obsession.

Nothing was going to keep me from claiming her before the eyes of God and man.

She's finally mine... and I'm never letting her go.

Vicious Oath

Damien & Yelena's story

When I give an order, I expect it to be obeyed.

She's too smart for her own good, and it's going to get her killed.

Against my better judgement, I put her under the protection of my powerful Russian mafia family.

So imagine my anger when the little minx ran.

For three long years I've been on her trail, always one step behind.

Finding and claiming her had become an obsession.

It was getting harder to rein in my driving need to possess her… to own her.

But now the chase is over.

I've found her.

Soon she will be mine.

And I plan to make it official, even if I have to drag her kicking and screaming to the altar.

This time… there will be no escape from me.

Betrayed Honor

Mikhail & Nadia's story

Her innocence was going to get her killed.

That was if I didn't get to her first.

She's the protected little sister of the powerful Ivanov Russian mafia family - the very definition of forbidden.

It's always been my job, as their Head of Security, to watch over her but never to touch.

That ends today.

She disobeyed me and put herself in danger.

It was time to take her in hand.

I'm the only one who can save her and I will fight anyone who tries to stop me, including her brothers.

Honor and loyalty be damned.

She's mine now.

DARK OBSESSION TRILOGY

A Dark Romantic Suspense

Ward

It should have been a fairytale...

A Billionaire Duke sweeps a poor American actress off her feet to a romantic,

isolated English estate.

A grand love affair... except this wasn't love.

It was obsession.

He had it all planned from the beginning, before I even knew he existed. He chose me.

I'm his unwilling captive, forced to play his sadistic game.

He is playing with my mind as well as my body.

Trying to convince me it is 1895, and I'm his obedient ward, subject to his rules and discipline.

Everywhere I look it is the Victorian era.

He says that my memories of a modern life are delusions

which need to be driven from my mind through punishment.

If I don't submit, he will send me back to the asylum.

I know it's not true... any of it... at least I think it's not.

The lines between reality and this nightmare are starting to blur.

If I don't escape now, I will be lost in his world forever.

It should have been a fairytale...

Gilded Cage

He's controlling, manipulative, dangerous...

and I'm in love with him.

Rich and powerful, Richard is used to getting whatever he wants... and he wants me.

This isn't a romance.

It's a dark and twisted obsession.

A game of ever-increasingly depraved acts.

Every time I fight it, he just pulls me deeper into his deception.

The slightest disobedience to his rules brings swift punishment.

My life as I knew it is gone.

He now controls everything.

I'm caught in his web, the harder I struggle, the more entangled I become.

I no longer know my own mind.

He owns my body, making me crave his painful touch.

But the worst deception of all?

He's made me love him.

If I don't break free soon, there will be no escape for me.

Toxic

In every story there is a hero and a villain... I'm both.

I will corrupt her beautiful innocence till her soul is as dark and twisted as my own.

With every caress, every taboo touch, I will captivate and ensnare her.

She's mine and no one is going to take her from me.

No matter how many times my little bird tries to escape, I will always give chase and bring her back to where she belongs, in my arms.

Each time she defies me, the consequences become more deadly.

I may not be the hero she wanted, but I'm the man she needs.

For a list of All of Zoe Blake's Books Visit her Website!

www.zblakebooks.com

VIP Tip: There are several bonus books listed on her website!

THANK YOU!

Stormy Night Publications would like to thank you for your interest in our books.

If you liked this book (or even if you didn't), we would really appreciate you leaving a review on the site where you purchased it. Reviews provide useful feedback for us and our authors, and this feedback (both positive comments and constructive criticism) allows us to work even harder to make sure we provide the content our customers want to read.

If you would like to check out more books from Stormy Night Publications, if you want to learn more about our company, or if you would like to join our mailing list, please visit our website at:
http://www.stormynightpublications.com

Printed in Great Britain
by Amazon